ONE MAN'S POISON

JOHN R. RIGGS

ONE MAN'S POISON

DEMBNER BOOKS
New York

For Red Dembner

A Dembner Book

Published by Barricade Books, Inc.,
61 Fourth Avenue, New York, N.Y. 10003

Distributed by W. W. Norton & Company, Inc.,
500 Fifth Avenue, New York, N.Y. 10110

Library of Congress Cataloging-in-Publication Data
Riggs, John R., 1945–
    One man's poison / by John R. Riggs.
        p.   cm. — (A Garth Ryland mystery)
    ISBN 0-942637-31-3
    I. Title. II. Series: Riggs, John R., 1945–
Garth Ryland mystery.
PS3568.I372O54   1991
813'.54—dc20   90-35745
                                                      CIP

Design by Antler & Baldwin, Inc.
Second Printing, April 1991

1

March came in like a lamb on the heels of a gentle south wind that fattened the willows and redbuds and filled the air with thaw. For a week the mild weather held. I saw my first robin, heard my first geese, found my first crocus along the south wall of the small concrete-block building that housed the *Oakalla Reporter*, and smiled my first big smile of spring. Then the wind swung sharply to the northwest, froze my footprints in the mud outside my office window, and tightened winter's noose once more.

Ruth was standing by the stove when the earthquake hit. I was sitting at the kitchen table. We both thought that it was a gust of wind that rattled the house and shook her potted ivy from the shelf. The next morning we learned that all of central Wisconsin, from as far north as Stevens Point to as far south as Janesville, had felt the tremor. Except for a few cracked windows and some broken dishes, the quake had done little damage in Oakalla, where we lived. But for those of us landlubbers who thought we were safely tucked away from earthquakes there in the heartland of America, each succeeding aftershock left us less sure of

1

ourselves—especially the second day after the quake when Oakalla's water went bad.

The earthquake had come on a Thursday night. The next Thursday morning I sat in my office at my oak desk, writing my syndicated column for Friday's edition of the *Oakalla Reporter*, a small weekly newspaper that I'd owned and edited for eight years. I'd bought the *Oakalla Reporter* with the money willed to me by Grandmother Ryland and moved to Oakalla from Milwaukee, where I'd previously worked as managing editor of the *Milwaukee Journal*. In Milwaukee I'd left behind a former wife, a son whose grave I still couldn't visit, and a large part of me that I no longer recognized, even in retrospect. It seemed that while I had lived in other places, I hadn't really begun to live until I moved to Oakalla. Part of it had to do with owning my own business and being my own boss. But most of it, I thought, had to do with Oakalla itself and the people who lived there. Even as a boy I knew it was a special place to visit, and I always looked forward to my summers at Grandmother Ryland's farm. What I didn't realize then, and what I'd come to realize, was that in Oakalla I'd found a home.

Rupert Roberts came into my office, walked past my desk without a hello, and stood staring out the window. Tall and gaunt, and the only three-term sheriff in the history of Adams County, he rarely smiled and spoke with a drawl that never once got in a hurry. We'd been friends ever since he'd shown me the ropes shortly after I'd moved to Oakalla. He was sixty-three years old. That morning he looked it.

"And a good morning to you too," I said.

Ignoring me, he continued to stare out the window. "Did anyone ever tell you, Garth, about how when it rains, it pours?"

"I've heard it said. Why?"

He reached into his pocket, took out the tobacco

2

pouch that his wife, Elvira, had given him, pinched off a chew, and put the pouch back into his pocket. Meanwhile I cut the top out of an empty Coke can and handed it to him to spit in. "Much obliged," he said, turning back to the window.

"You going to tell me or not?" I asked.

"Tell you what?"

"Whatever it is that's got you down."

He pulled away from the window and sat down on a chair opposite me. I noticed that his face was white and pinched, as if he were in pain, and the usual humor in his eyes was gone.

"Are you all right?" I asked.

"Why wouldn't I be?" he said, spitting into the Coke can.

"You look a little pale to me."

"I am a little pale," he replied. "I haven't felt quite up to par lately."

"In what way not up to par?" I asked.

Taking off his hat, he brushed it a couple times with his hand before resting it on his knee. "That's not what I came in here for," he said. "To talk about me."

"Then what did you come in here for?"

"I need your help," he said. "Rowena Parker called me a few minutes ago to tell me Jimmy Parker was missing."

"I thought she and Jimmy were divorced." At least that's what she'd told me.

"They are."

"Then what's the concern?" I asked.

He took a moment to answer. "Little Jimmy Parker, Rowena's son, is supposedly with him."

"How long have they been missing?" I asked.

"At least since last Sunday," he answered, picking up his hat from the chair and adjusting the brim. "Jimmy senior was supposed to have Jimmy junior back

3

to Rowena by late Sunday evening. *But* he never made
it."

"This is Thursday," I pointed out.

"I know that."

"Why did she wait until now to call?"

"She didn't say."

"Didn't or wouldn't?"

He gave me a look intended to put me in my place.
"I can't see how that matters, since it amounts to the
same thing."

"Just asking," I said.

He shook his head as if to reprimand himself. "I'm
sorry, Garth. Your question was on line. But for now I'm
not going to answer it."

"Fair enough," I said, though I wondered why he
was holding out on me. "Is there anything you can tell
me, like where big Jimmy might have taken little
Jimmy?"

"Rowena doesn't know for sure. But she thinks to
an Indian dig somewhere. That's where they usually go
on weekends."

"That could be anywhere," I said.

"Agreed." He rose and started for the door.

"You said when it rains, it pours."

"What was that?" He seemed distracted. I noticed
sweat on his forehead.

"You said earlier that when it rains, it pours. What
else is wrong besides the fact that big and little Jimmy
Parker might be missing?"

He took his still fresh chew out of his mouth and
put it into the Coke can. "You know how the water
smelled and tasted last Saturday morning after the
earthquake on Thursday, like rotten eggs or worse?
Well, to be on the safe side I took a sample of it and sent
it to the State Board of Health. The results came back
yesterday. Besides the hydrogen sulfide, which is what's

4

making it taste so bad, and a lot of other things that don't count, our water's got a trace of cyanide in it."

"How much of a trace?" I asked.

"So many parts per million," he answered, "if that. It's not enough to hurt anybody yet, but it could if it gets more concentrated."

"You have any idea where the cyanide is coming from?" I asked.

"No."

"Could somebody deliberately be putting the cyanide in the water?"

His jaw tightened. He didn't seem to want to consider that possibility. "I don't see how. Clarkie and I have the only two keys to the pump house, and for the life of me I can't see Clarkie doing it."

Clarkie was Chief Deputy Harold Clark, who was as likely to poison Oakalla's water as Rupert was. "That must mean it's coming from an outside source."

"That's the way I've got it figured too," he agreed.

"Is that what you want my help on, finding out how the cyanide's getting in our water?" I asked.

"No. That can wait. What I want you to do is to help me find little Jimmy Parker." Something in the way he said it made it seem that even more was at stake than a missing boy.

"I can't do anything today," I said. "Maybe tomorrow."

"Tomorrow will be soon enough." Though I could tell that he wished it were today.

"Why?" I asked before he could leave.

"Why what?"

"Why are you asking for my help in this, instead of taking care of it yourself?"

He stared past me at the window and the day outside. "You want an honest answer?" he said. "Because I don't feel up to it."

"Physically or otherwise?"

"Does it matter?" he asked.

5

"I guess not," I said, disappointed that he wouldn't tell me. "But there is one thing I do need to know," I continued. "How many other people know about the missing Jimmy Parkers besides you and me?"

He took a sudden deep breath, held it a moment, then let it out. "Whoever Rowena Parker has told."

"You haven't spread the word?"

He abruptly turned to leave. "I'm on my way, Garth." But he had to stop at the door and hold on.

"You sure you're all right?"

"I'll make it," he answered.

"That's not what I asked."

"I know that," he said on his way out.

I watched him all the way to his patrol car, where he rested a moment before leaving. Then I made a phone call to his wife, Elvira, but she wasn't home. After several more phone calls I still hadn't tracked her down, so I settled for Clarkie, whom I caught at home.

"Clarkie, this is Garth. I'm worried about Rupert. He was in my office a few minutes ago, looking and acting like death warmed over. You have any idea what's the matter with him?"

"Nope," Clarkie said, sounding concerned. "He was fine late last evening when I saw him."

"Well, keep your eye on him for me, will you? And let me know what happens."

"Will do," he promised.

I hung up and sat there for a few minutes staring out the window. I knew that Rupert wouldn't back off from anything without a good reason, or ask me to help him unless he truly believed that he couldn't do the job himself. Still, he had come to me for help. That worried me.

After spending the rest of the morning working on the *Oakalla Reporter*, I walked to the Corner Bar and Grill for lunch. After a week of wind and rain, the day

6

was cool and serene. The sky was blue, streaked with high white strands of cirrus that looked more like smoke than clouds. A cardinal sang his heart out from the top of a cedar tree. A large flock of geese passed overhead, breaking formation as first one and then another took his turn at the lead. A cow bawled for her calf somewhere south of the old Nickelplate line. A mourning dove drowsed and nodded in the warm noonday sun, taking no notice of me as I went by.

Parked along the south side of Jackson Street beside the Corner Bar and Grill was a dark-blue 1955 Chevy pickup with rusted 1955 Montana license plates front and back, a homemade camper shell in its bed, and enough dings and dents all over it to qualify it for the Demolition Derby. Still wearing its original paint, which had dulled but not flaked over the years, the pickup had traveled many miles over dusty roads before reaching Oakalla, and, judging from the dust imbedded in the paint itself, probably many hundreds of miles over dusty roads before that.

Normally at lunchtime the Corner Bar and Grill reverberated with loud talk and laughter, as we regulars tried to make ourselves heard over the jukebox and each other. But that day only whispers broke the silence as I entered and sat at the counter. Three seats down from me I saw the reason for the silence. A stranger sat in our midst.

Dressed in black jeans, black boots, and a black ten-gallon hat, he wore a black cotton shirt with pearl buttons, a black string tie with a turquoise clasp, and a black leather belt with a turquoise buckle. He had large thick ears, a large hooked nose, solemn black eyes, and a presence that filled the room. I couldn't take my eyes off of him. He seemed not to notice me.

Giving the stranger a wide berth, Bernice Phillips, the co-owner of the Corner Bar and Grill, came up to take my order. "What'll it be, Garth?" she asked.

"A cheeseburger with fried onions and a glass of chocolate milk," I answered. The man three stools down looked my way. I smiled. He didn't smile back.

"That all, Garth?" Bernice asked.

The man turned back to his coffee. I turned to look at Bernice. "Unless you have any pecan pie left."

She nodded to the man on my left. "He ate the last two pieces."

Again giving the stranger a wide berth, Bernice took my order to the kitchen. Meanwhile, Sniffy Smith came in and took a seat at the counter between the stranger and me. Sniffy had officially retired from barbering a few years before and only cut hair on Fridays, and then only when the spirit moved him. I was one of the favored few of his old customers who still got their haircuts from him—a dubious honor at best.

"Afternoon, Garth," Sniffy said, eyeing the stranger. "Why is it so damn quiet in here? Did somebody die or something?"

I nodded in the stranger's direction. "I think it has something to do with him," I said.

"Why's that?" Sniffy asked, picking up a cold french fry off the counter and eating it. "Ain't nobody in here ever seen a real live Indian before." Then he turned to the stranger. "Howdy, Chief," he said, extending his hand. "I'm Sniffy Smith. This here's Garth Ryland, the man to ask if there's anything you want to know about Oakalla."

The stranger didn't even raise an eyebrow in reply. When it became obvious to everyone in the Corner Bar and Grill that he wasn't going to reply, Sniffy slowly withdrew his hand, sniffed a couple times in indignation, and said loudly enough for everyone to hear, "And I was just about to offer you a free haircut too."

That broke the ice. Though the stranger didn't laugh, everyone else in the place did, and soon things

8

were almost back to normal again. Sniffy, however, still feeling the sting of rejection, swiveled his seat around and sat with his back to the stranger.

"You doing anything tomorrow night?" Sniffy asked a few minutes later as I drank the last of my chocolate milk.

"Not that I know of. Why?"

"I need an euchre partner."

"What's the matter with Herb Felix?" Herb was Sniffy's usual euchre partner.

"He's going into the hospital to have some cataracts removed. I doubt he'll be back to normal by tomorrow night."

I thought it over. Playing partners with Sniffy in anything was like playing baseball at dusk. You pitched, prayed, and ducked in that order. "Sure. Why not," I said.

"And while you're at it," Sniffy said as I stopped at the cash register, "you might see what you can do to get this water right again. I'm getting tired of drinking pop."

The stranger's eyes turned toward me, as if intent on my answer. So did the eyes of several others. I felt as though I had to choose my words carefully. "Given time," I said, "I think the water will clear up on its own. It always has before."

"It's never been this bad before," Sniffy pointed out. "Not in my memory anyway, and I've lived here all my life."

"Nor in mine," I admitted, then left.

Throughout the afternoon and evening I worked on the *Oakalla Reporter*, finishing shortly before midnight when I called my printer in. I waited until the last paper came off the press before starting home under a clear, starry sky. When I was nearly there, someone drove by in a dark-blue 1955 Chevy pickup with Montana license plates, circled the block, waited for me to go inside, then parked along the street across from my house. With nothing better to do, I blinked my front porch light at him a couple times before climbing the stairs to bed.

2

The next morning Ruth Krammes, my housekeeper, and I sat across the kitchen table from each other, trying to drink our coffee, which, no matter how much cream and sugar I put into it, still tasted like rotten eggs to me. Ruth wore her ancient flowered pink robe, the fur-lined moccasins I'd given her Christmas before last, and a look of disgust. Somewhere between sixty and seventy, Ruth had been my housekeeper ever since I moved to Oakalla. She, along with a collection of her friends and relatives, had an information network that was second to none, and whenever I needed to know anything about Oakalla or its people, I just asked Ruth. Whenever I needed advice about my own personal problems, I just asked Ruth. And whenever I needed someone to commiserate with, I just asked Ruth, though she doled out sympathy with about the same fervor as Scrooge did one-hundred-dollar bills. About the only time I didn't ask Ruth for her advice was in those matters dealing with the *Oakalla Reporter*. There she gave it without my asking.

"I can't believe some people actually like this stuff," I said in reference to the artesian taste of the water. "Even go out of their way to buy it."

"Some people like snails and grasshoppers too." Then she looked right at me and said, "There's no accounting for taste."

I knew what she meant by that. It was only one of her many references to Diana in a long-standing disagreement between us. Ruth didn't approve of Diana, who up until recently had been the love of my life, and Ruth was not shy about letting me know that.

"It's been six months," I said, counting to myself. "More like seven, since she moved away."

"When you stop counting, that's when I'll stop worrying." She pushed her coffee to the other side of the table. "When's Rupert going to do something about the water? It's the worst it's ever been."

"Worse than you know," I said. "It's got cyanide in it."

Without saying a word she rose and dumped her coffee and mine into the sink, then poured out what was left in the coffeepot and rinsed it down the drain. "You might have told me sooner," she said.

"It's not supposed to be enough to hurt us. At least that's what the man at the State Board of Health told Rupert."

"What does he know?"

I shrugged. "You'll have to ask him."

She began rummaging through the cupboards for what turned out to be a can of cocoa. It had sat in there for so long she had to chisel it out of the can with a butter knife.

"What else did Rupert have to say?" she asked.

"He said that Jimmy Parker and his son were missing, and have been since last Sunday."

"Then why haven't we heard anything about it before now?"

"That's what I asked Rupert," I said. "He didn't seem to want to talk about it."

"Maybe with good reason," she answered.

12

I waited while she mixed some sugar with the cocoa, then set the mixture on the stove and added a little milk, stirring it in before adding the rest of the milk.

"You remember Rupert's youngest son, David, don't you?" she asked.

"I remember David," I answered. Next to Fran Baldwin, Diana's late husband, David Roberts was probably the most handsome, charming, and athletic man I'd ever known. He could do just about anything he set his mind to—ski, dance, surf, hang-glide, design a house, or rebuild a carburetor. And he did it all with an ease that made me envious.

At twenty-eight David Roberts had also been in and out of four different colleges and at least three different jails that I knew of. And he'd been in and out of so many different relationships, he once jokingly remarked that he needed a scorecard to keep track of them. He was the same way about friendships. One day you were his best buddy; the next day he might speak to you on the street if you spoke to him first, and then again he might not. You never knew with David. Like the cars he drove and the clothes he wore, most of the people in his life were expendable.

Still, I liked David Roberts. With his natural grace and charm, it was hard not to like him. And I might have liked him even better if I hadn't seen him walking out of Diana's back door early one summer morning four years ago when Fran was out of town and Diana and I were just friends.

"I thought you might remember David," Ruth said, knowing more than I wanted her to. Leave it to Ruth to remind me that not all of the past battles I'd fought had been won.

"What does David have to do with it?" I asked.

"You know he's back in town?"

"I know I've seen him around, but I didn't think

much about it. Where's he staying, with Rupert and Elvira?"

She gave me a look that said I should know better. "After Rupert kicked him out of the house the last time he was home and told him never to come back? What do you think?"

"Where is he staying then?" I asked.

"With Rowena Parker," she said.

I felt my chest tighten. Rowena Parker was Jimmy Parker's former wife, little Jimmy Parker's mother, and a recent acquaintance of mine. "I'm beginning to get the picture," I said.

Ruth put the carton of milk back into the refrigerator. "What you may or may not realize," she continued, "is that this is not the first time the two of them have hooked up. Rowena was seeing David before he left town to go to college for the last time. It was shortly after that that she married Jimmy Parker." After pouring a cup of cocoa for me and one for herself, she sat back down at the table. "There's some question in some of our minds as to who little Jimmy's father really is."

I sipped the cocoa, burning my tongue as I did. "Rowena never mentioned that to me."

"Mentioned what to you?"

"That she and David used to go together. She talked a lot about herself and what she'd been through, but she hardly ever mentioned Jimmy, except in passing, and she never mentioned David."

Ruth's brows rose like antennae, the way they did whenever she thought she was on to something. "And when did you and Rowena Parker get so chummy?"

I shook my head. "It's not important. Besides, it's over." I took another sip of cocoa. "If it ever really began."

"Your ears are turning red," she observed.

"Are they? I hadn't noticed."

Taking a sip of her cocoa, Ruth grimaced, then set

the cup back down again. "How can you sit there and drink that?" she said. "It tastes like a three-year-old Easter rabbit."

"What's my alternative?" I asked. Then I remembered something that I'd forgotten to ask her. "What do you know about Rupert's health?"

"What do you mean, What do I know about Rupert's health? He might not look it, but he's as healthy as a horse and always has been."

"He wasn't yesterday morning," I said. "He seemed in real pain, and I don't think it had anything to do with either the water or the fact that Rowena Parker's son, who is maybe Rupert's grandson, is missing."

Ruth looked concerned. Rupert was one of the few people in Oakalla that she genuinely liked. "I haven't heard anything about him," she said. "But I'll look into it if you want me to."

"I want you to."

When I stepped outside my door a few minutes later, I saw an old blue Chevy pickup pull away from the curb and head uptown. It was parked in front of the Corner Bar and Grill when I walked by there. Its driver waited for me to pass before he went inside.

Rowena Parker lived on the south side of Jackson Street in a small white bungalow that needed only some imagination and a fresh coat of paint to make it look as good as new again. Clumps of bluegrass, some taller and thicker than others, probably compliments of the neighbor's dog, dotted the yard, and a forgotten snow shovel along with a red tricycle were parked in the shrubbery in front of the house. Above the side door to Rowena's beauty shop hung a wooden sign that read SNIP AND SWIRL. Looking through the door into her shop, I didn't see anyone there.

But Rowena Parker answered the doorbell on the third ring. A tall, dark-haired beauty who had inherited

15

the shop from her mother, Rowena had large dark-brown eyes, thin dark eyebrows kept in perfect trim, a cleft in her chin, and a mole on her right cheek. She wore jeans, no makeup that I could see, a man's flannel shirt, and the look of someone who'd have rather been left alone.

"I'm closed today," she said from inside the shop.

"I see you are," I said. "But I'm not here for a haircut."

"Then why are you here?"

"Sheriff Roberts asked me to help him find your son. That's why I'm here."

She hesitated, glanced over her shoulder at something, then opened the door so I could come inside. The smell that greeted me was an old and familiar one from the days of my childhood when Eddie Babb and I used to take a shortcut through his mother's beauty shop on our way outside to play. I never liked the smell then. I still didn't like the smell. But I hadn't forgotten it.

"I don't know what I can tell you that I haven't already told Sheriff Roberts," she said. "So you're probably wasting your time, *Mr. Ryland.*"

I had that coming. A couple of months after Diana left for New Mexico, which was a few months after Rowena and Jimmy Parker were divorced, and before David Roberts came back to Oakalla, Rowena and I had spent several nights together at the Corner Bar and Grill, telling each other our troubles. Then, partly because I wanted to quit spending so many of my nights at the Corner Bar and Grill and partly because I didn't know where to go from there, I'd quit seeing Rowena. I'd never told her why. I had intended to, but somehow I just never got around to it. Grandmother Ryland would have called me a coward for that.

"Have I come at a bad time?" I asked.

She stood stiffly in front of me with her jaw set and her hands on her hips, as if she couldn't quite decide whether to punch me or spit on me. "Not at a bad time, Mr. Ryland. Not at a good time either. I just don't like people who go prying into other people's business like you do."

"You called Sheriff Roberts to say your son, Jimmy, was missing," I answered. "He asked me to help find him. If you call that prying, then you have a right not to like me."

"That's not what I mean," she said. "And you know it."

I knew what she meant, but with David Roberts standing in the doorway behind her, I didn't think this was the time to discuss it. "Hello, David," I said.

"Hello, Garth," he said with a smile.

Rowena Parker looked first at David, then at me. "Do you two know each other?" she asked.

I answered, "We've met."

"More than met," David added. "Actually, Garth and I are old friends. He even saved my life once."

Rowena stood helplessly between us, deflated by our exchange. "Why don't I fix us all a cup of coffee," she said.

"That's not necessary," I said. "I'm not staying. I just came to ask you a couple of questions, that's all. Then I'll leave you in peace."

"You might as well stay for coffee," David offered. "It's the least we can do for an old friend." Lounging lazily in the doorway, wearing jeans and a black T-shirt stretched tightly across his broad chest, David's confident pose told the same old story. But something in his cool blue eyes said that things had changed between us. Though he continued to smile, I could see the effort behind it.

"Thanks, but no thanks," I said.

"Then ask your questions and leave us alone," Rowena said, her anger returning.

David Roberts shrugged at me as if to say he'd done

all he could in the matter. I had seen the same look eight years ago when I had dragged him out of his overturned black Camaro just seconds before it exploded. It didn't seem to matter to him then, as it didn't matter to him now, what I did or didn't do, only that he not break faith with himself, or with whoever he perceived himself to be.

"Okay," I said. "Question number one. If Jimmy was supposed to be back home on Sunday as promised, why did you wait until Thursday to tell someone?"

"I'm afraid that's my fault, Garth," David interrupted before Rowena had a chance to answer. "Rowena wanted to call as early as Sunday night. I was the one who told her to wait."

"Why?" I asked.

"Because Jimmy Parker is a flake," Rowena found her voice. "When he says Sunday, he might mean Tuesday, or the next Saturday, depending on where he goes and what he finds at one of those digs of his. I can't tell you the number of times I've sat up nights wondering just where my son was. Or the number of times I've had to call the school to say that Jimmy won't be in kindergarten today."

"Then why did you call on Thursday when you knew it might be Saturday before Jimmy came home?" I asked. "Have you ever called anyone before to report him missing?"

Rowena and David exchanged glances. Apparently neither one of them wanted to answer that question. "No," Rowena finally said.

"Why not?" I asked.

"I told you why not," she said. "My former husband is a flake. You can't depend on him for anything. And if I pressed him too hard, he might take Jimmy and just disappear."

"Do you think that's what happened this time?"

"I don't know," she answered, looking to David for help.

"Then why did you call Sheriff Roberts?"

"Because I told her to," David said.

"Why?"

"How would it look," he asked, "if she hadn't?"

"How would what look?" I asked.

For a second time they exchanged glances. "In case something really did happen to him," he answered. "What kind of mother would Rowena be then?" Seeing the hurt on her face, he added, "In the eyes of Oakalla, I mean."

"I would think," I answered evenly, trying to keep my temper, "that I wouldn't be too worried about appearances in a case like this."

"Goddamn you!" Rowena exploded, her dark eyes flashing. "What gives you the right to judge me? How do you know what I've been through these past five years?" Then she looked away, because I did know a lot of what she'd been through the past five years. She'd told me so herself.

"I think I know you well enough not to expect this," I said.

"Screw you!" she shouted. She turned to David. "And screw you too. I told you we shouldn't let him into the house." She pushed him aside on her way out of the room.

"Women," he shrugged, following her into the living room and leaving me alone in the beauty shop.

From there I walked to the Marathon service station where Danny Palmer, the owner of the Marathon, stood in the drive pumping gas. Danny loved his work. You could tell by the spring in his step and the smile on his face. He didn't walk from the station to your car to see what you needed. He ran. When he wasn't pumping gas, he was washing windshields, changing oil, rotating tires, tuning engines, and running a wrecker service on

19

the side. About the only thing he wouldn't do was wash and wax your car. Or whistle while he worked. Even Danny had his limits.

"Morning, Garth," Danny said, using a rag to wipe the oil from his hands. "What can I do for you?"

"I'm looking for Jimmy Parker. I wondered if you'd seen him recently."

He stuffed his rag back into the hip pocket of his coveralls. "Not recently. He stopped by for a fill-up one day late last week."

"Which day, do you remember?" I asked.

"Saturday I believe it was." Leon Metzger honked and waved as he drove by. Danny and I both waved back. "He was in here looking for Judge Glick. Asking if I'd seen him lately."

"Have you seen him lately?" The Judge Glick whom I knew had suffered a severe stroke a couple of years before. Though I hadn't printed his obituary, I often wondered if he was still alive.

"A month or so ago," Danny said. "He came in for an oil change. It was the first time I'd seen him since his stroke. I hardly recognized him."

We walked to the door of his station. Sniffy Smith sat on his favorite stool inside reading Danny's *Oakalla Reporter*. "What did Jimmy Parker want with Judge Glick, you have any idea?" I asked.

"No," Danny answered.

"Has Jimmy been before Judge Glick in the past?"

"Not that I know of."

We waved at another honking car. Then I asked, "Was little Jimmy with him when Jimmy was in here?"

Danny nodded. "Jimmy bought two candy bars and a case of Cokes."

"A case of Cokes? Why so many?"

Danny shrugged on his way inside. "I never thought to ask."

20

3

Judge Thorton Glick lived on the west side of Fair Haven Road at the north end of town between Edgar Shoemaker's welding shop on one side and Stub Timmons' salvage yard on the other. Weather-stained and vine-covered, the two-story, orange-brick house was surrounded by shrubs and ornamental cedars that seemed to spread and thicken every year, covering ever more of the house until it was hard to see the bricks behind them. White wooden pillars supported a narrow front porch, and two high, steep gables were joined by a slate roof whose gutters had rusted through in several places and bled onto the bricks below. Behind the house stood a small gray barn ensnarled in vines as thick as my wrist. Along Fair Haven Road in front of the house lay a dead cat.

His long white hair gnarled and matted, the cat had his two front legs stretched out stiffly in front of him and his two back legs stretched out stiffly behind, as if he'd been hit in full stride while racing for the sidewalk. A big cat, he wore a look of confidence on his face, as if he fully expected to reach the sidewalk as he had so many times in the past.

I bent down to drag him off the edge of the road

21

when someone said, "Don't bother. He ain't your problem."

I looked up to see Stub Timmons standing on the sidewalk a few feet away. A squat bearlike man with a grizzled growth of beard, small greedy eyes, and Popeye forearms, Stub Timmons affected me that day the same as he always had. Instantly my breath caught in my throat, my adrenaline kicked in, and I was ready to do battle. I didn't know why I reacted so strongly, since to my knowledge neither Stub Timmons nor I had ever spoken that first harsh word to the other. Maybe it was instinct, a holdover from the days when the Rylands wore animal skins, carried clubs, bashed first, and asked questions later. Because whenever our paths crossed, Stub Timmons brought out the Neanderthal in me.

Stub brushed past me, picked up the cat, and threw him in the general direction of his property. The cat landed in a puddle of rainwater, scattering some English sparrows that had gathered there to drink.

Stub laughed. "Bet they ain't never seen a flying cat before."

"Probably not," I agreed.

A momentary silence followed. Stub stood his ground like he was rooted there. I stood on one foot and then the other, trying to keep my toes warm. Though I thought I was dressed for the weather, the wind had found the holes in my tennis shoes.

"What are you doing up in this neck of the woods?" Stub asked. "It ain't like you to be nosing around somewhere without some purpose in mind." The question seemed innocent enough, but I didn't take it that way.

"I came to see Judge Glick."

"What about?" Though he smiled broadly, I noticed Stub's fists were clenched.

"That's between Judge Glick and me. It's nobody's business but ours."

22

After using his thumb to blow his nose, Stub then wiped his hand on his coveralls. "You're wasting your time trying to talk to the Judge about anything. After his stroke he ain't had much of a mind left, that or anything else."

I shrugged. "I'll just have to take my chances then."

Stub edged a step closer, close enough for me to smell the motor oil on him. "You ain't listening to me, Ryland. I'm trying to tell you the Judge ain't in no shape to talk to anyone. So why don't you go on back to the other end of town where you belong."

"I didn't realize I'd crossed the Mason-Dixon line," I said.

Stub smiled. "Hell, I didn't mean it that way, Ryland. What I meant was you're wasting your time here. You might as well be spending it where it'll do you some good." I glimpsed something beneath his smile that frightened me. "Like that writing you're so good at."

"Got a light, Stub," Edgar Shoemaker said, sticking his cigar within an inch of Stub Timmons' nose. Stub and I had been so engrossed in each other we hadn't seen Edgar coming.

"The goddamn thing is already lit, Edgar," Stub said, backing away. "When are you going to get some glasses, like I've been telling you to."

Edgar took his cigar out of his mouth and examined it. "Well, I'll be damned, Stub," he said, sounding surprised. "It is lit. I thought it had gone out on me again." Then Edgar turned to me and offered his hand. "Long time no see, Garth," he said. "It is Garth, isn't it?"

Blind in one eye, and partially blind in the other one, Edgar Shoemaker could still outweld anyone in Adams County and had a long-standing reputation that brought him specialty work from places as distant as Green Bay and Eau Claire. Edgar and I had been friends for many years and had once restored a 1936

Cadillac together. Though when we sat around his Franklin stove and talked old times, the Cadillac was one thing we didn't mention.

"It's Garth," I said, shaking his hand. "How have you been, Edgar?"

"I can't complain. Though I'm getting a little sick of winter along about now."

"That makes two of us."

Stub Timmons abruptly left in the direction of his salvage yard. "Don't go thinking you'll be missed," Edgar yelled.

Stub didn't answer, but went inside his building and slammed the door behind him.

"So what *are* you doing up in this neck of the woods?" Edgar asked me. "It wouldn't have anything to do with anything, would it?"

"It might."

"Then why don't you come inside and warm up. You can fill me in on all you've been up to lately."

"I'd love to, Edgar," I said. "But I have a feeling that this isn't going to be my last stop of the day."

"Long enough to thaw your toes at least?"

I smiled at him. "I guess I have that long."

We went inside his welding shop where Edgar stoked his Franklin stove until it began to glow. Then he fixed us each a cup of instant coffee, handing me a plastic spoon, which I used to add sugar and powdered milk. I cautiously tasted the coffee, then smiled in relief. It didn't taste anything at all like the coffee Ruth and I had earlier that morning.

"What's your secret?" I asked him. "You beat everybody else to the spring water at Heavin's Market?"

He sucked hard on his cigar, trying to get it to go. When it wouldn't, he laid it on top of his welding stool and stood with his hands over the stove to warm them. "I've got my own well," he said.

"So do I," I said. "But that doesn't seem to help any."

24

"Yours a deep or a shallow well?" he asked.

"Deep. It goes down about two hundred and ten feet."

Turning to warm the back side of him, he said, "That's the difference. Mine is a ground water cistern. It probably doesn't run any deeper than twenty feet, if that." He nodded in the direction of Stub Timmons' salvage yard. "Of course, with Stub in the neighborhood that's not usually something to brag about."

"I've heard Stub's not too particular about what goes in there," I said.

Warmed on both sides, Edgar picked up his cigar, lighted it with his welding torch, and sat down on his stool. "You might say that. That's probably where that cat of his will go once he gets around to it. If he gets around to it," he added. "A couple summers ago he once let a dog lie there in front of his place for two weeks. It got to stinking so bad that even the buzzards wouldn't come around anymore."

I looked down at my coffee, then at Edgar. "You ever had your water tested?"

He took a satisfied look around his shop. "A couple, three times in the years I've lived here. Of course, they condemned it each time for one reason or another. But since I rarely drink it unless I boil it, I try not to let it worry me."

"Remind me of that when you offer me lemonade this summer."

Edgar smiled, leaning back on his stool. "I make that at home out of my deep-water well. Of course, if the water don't clear up soon, there won't be many of us making lemonade this summer."

"Strange, isn't it," I said, fixed on a thought. "How your well and my well and the city wells all taste the same. You'd think they might by chance be fed by different sources, but apparently they aren't."

"Must be like oil wells," Edgar said in reply. "One

pool feeds all of them. And when it runs sour, they all do."

"That makes sense," I agreed, turning to cook the back of me before I went outside again. "And while I hate to drink and run, I'd better get on my way."

"Anywhere in particular?" Edgar asked.

"Judge Glick's. I was on my way there when Stub intercepted me."

Edgar leaned forward on his stool. "What do you need to see Judge Glick about?" he asked. "It wouldn't have anything to do with Jimmy Parker, would it? I hear he's missing."

It was my turn to smile. "Word travels fast in Oakalla."

"Sometimes. It depends on who you know."

"But why would I want to ask Judge Glick about Jimmy Parker?" I said. "I didn't even know they knew each other."

"Jimmy's done some work for the Judge in the past," he said. "I figured that's what Jimmy was up to last Saturday when he stopped by there. But he didn't stay long enough to do any work."

"You're sure it was Jimmy?" Edgar couldn't see as far away as Judge Glick's. Both he and I knew that.

"I didn't see him, if that's what you mean. But I'd know that El Camino of his anywhere, especially now that he's got a hole in his muffler."

"I wonder what he wanted with Judge Glick."

"Beats me. But you might ask the Judge when you see him."

"Thanks, Edgar, I plan to." At the door I stopped to ask, "You have any idea why Stub Timmons might not want me to see Judge Glick?"

Edgar slid down off his stool and picked up a welding rod. "The Judge is sort of an institution around here. That might explain some of it. But," he continued, lighting his welding torch, which spat a blue-green flame my way, "I can't figure out why he was coming on quite so strong on you in particular. You and Stub have words in the past?"

"Not that I know of. Maybe he just doesn't like me on general principles."

Edgar fine-tuned the flame and went to work on the frame he was building. "It's been known to happen."

Judge Glick took his time in answering his door. When he did answer it, I had to momentarily look away to hide my surprise. I remembered him as tall, straight, and fair with an unruly shock of ash-blond hair and deep green eyes that were at once both stern and compassionate. The man before me was frail, white, and whipsawed, bent to the point of breaking by something that had dashed his confidence and left him without hope. He reminded me of an old thoroughbred who, because of a cruel run of bad luck, had been forced in his last few years to pull a log wagon.

"Do I know you?" he asked, blinking at me with red watery eyes.

"I'm Garth Ryland. I publish the *Oakalla Reporter*."

"Of course," he said, reprimanding himself. "I should have known."

"Do you mind if I come in?" I asked.

He seemed puzzled, as if he couldn't quite grasp me yet. "Why would you want to come in?"

"To talk to you."

"What about?" he asked.

"It's about Jimmy Parker," I said.

That hit home. He pulled himself erect, looking more like the Judge Glick I remembered. "Jimmy Parker." He stepped aside to let me in. "Of course, Jimmy Parker."

I followed him into the parlor, which also served as a library for some of his rare books. Set in the southeast corner of the house, it had an east bay window with lace

27

curtains that looked out on Fair Haven Road, a puce-and-cream oriental rug on its oak floor, another bay window on the south wall with a fern stand and a fern in front of it, a high domed ceiling, and a red-tile fireplace that matched the puce in the rug. Judge Glick sat down in a studded brown leather chair facing the fireplace. I pulled up a matching brown leather chair beside him. Together we watched gas flames lick an artificial log.

"I like this room," I said for something to say. I liked the way the sunlight poured in through its east window and burned a white patch on the floor, and I liked its texture and its colors, the way it looked and the way it felt. Unlike a lot of houses that were bright on the outside and dim on the inside, Judge Glick's was just the opposite. No snarl of vines and shrubbery could totally block the beauty of its design.

"This was my father's favorite room," he answered with a brief sparkle in his eyes. "It used to be his study, where he'd prepare his briefs before going to court." The sparkle left his eyes. "It used to be mine too. But I hardly use it anymore."

"Your father was a lawyer?" I asked.

"My father was a *judge*," he corrected me. "Like his father before him." He stared vacantly at the fire. "Three generations of judges have lived in this house. There won't be a fourth."

Unmarried, with his sister, Isabelle, his only family, Thorton Glick had served as circuit court judge for nearly forty years. During most of that time he had been Oakalla's most prominent citizen, starring in the summer productions of the Oakalla Players, leading Oakalla's homecoming parade every year, and speaking on a myriad of subjects at the various clubs and organizations around town, all to the delight of his listeners. Then a few years ago, five by my calculations, he had suddenly quit the bench and become a virtual recluse. No one knew exactly why. But most of us in Oakalla felt it had

28

"What do you remember then?" I was annoyed with him. I felt like I was talking to a petulant child.

He stood, pulling himself fully erect. Looking up at him, at his lean craggy face and into his suddenly stern green eyes, I knew how the accused must have felt as he approached the bench. Justice, not mercy, would be his lot.

"Good day, young man," he said.

Outside, Stub Timmons stood in the doorway of his building watching as a new beige pickup pulled into his drive and two men got out. Stub took a long look at me before motioning the two men inside the building and closing the door behind them. Meanwhile I studied the pickup. I hadn't seen it in Oakalla before. Because of the emblem on its door and the tarp-covered cargo it carried, I guessed it was somebody's company truck, come to make a deposit at Stub's.

I didn't hear Judge Glick's gold Cadillac until he was halfway out of his drive. In an obvious hurry to get somewhere, he sped past me and turned north onto Fair Haven Road without even a glance to see if anyone might be coming. That brought Stub out of his building on the run. He got halfway to his rusty white pickup when he saw me still standing there. Abruptly he slowed to a walk before getting inside the pickup. But instead of driving away as he apparently wanted to do, he sat inside the pickup glaring at me until one of us had to give. It turned out to be Stub, who got out of the pickup and went back into the building. After waiting in vain for several minutes for him to come out of the building again, I started down Fair Haven Road toward town.

I met Rupert in his patrol car a couple of blocks later. "Give me a ride?" I said.

"Where to?"

"North on Fair Haven Road. I'd like to catch up with Judge Glick if we can."

"Any particular reason?

something to do with his sister, Isabelle, and whatever it was that led him to order her from their childhood home after a lifetime of living together, and to force her to set up residence in the ramshackle house directly across from him on Fair Haven Road.

"You mentioned Jimmy Parker," he said. "What about Jimmy Parker?"

"We have word that he's missing," I said. "I was wondering if you knew where he might have gone."

He seemed either unable or unwilling to lift his eyes from the hypnotic flames of the fire. "Why are you asking me?"

"Because I have it from a good source that he stopped by here briefly last Saturday. As far as I know, he hasn't been seen since."

I was watching him closely. The longer we talked, the more he seemed to draw ever deeper into himself. "If he did stop by here, I have since forgotten," he said. "My stroke, you see, has erased a lot of memories."

But not all of his memories, I observed. He remembered something only too well. It took all of his concentration.

"You remembered Jimmy Parker well enough a few minutes ago," I said. "Otherwise, why did you let me in here when I mentioned his name?"

He didn't answer.

"Judge Glick?"

He turned to me in anger. "Young man, do you have any idea whom you're talking to. I won't be questioned like a common criminal, especially in my own home."

"Nobody said anything about a crime, Judge Glick. But Jimmy Parker and his son are missing. If you know something about it, that's not something you should keep to yourself. There are other people to consider. Little Jimmy's mother in particular."

"And I told you I don't remember their being here.

4

We were down to our last two cards. Through a combination of luck, more luck, and Sniffy's unflagging optimism, we were tied for second place and one point out of first. This last hand of the night would either make or break us, since Bill Seager and Bob Marshall, who were leading the round of euchre, were also our opponents.

Sniffy, as dealer, had picked up the ten of hearts. He'd used that card to trump Bill Seager's lead of the ace of diamonds. Sniffy then led the jack of diamonds, or the left bower, and when it took the trick, he sniffed loudly enough for everyone else in the room to hear.

I knew what he was thinking. Flush from the moment and the uncanny run of luck we'd had all night, he was playing for all the tricks, two points, and victory. Slapping down the ace of hearts with the full expectation of taking the trick and claiming the hand, Sniffy was dismayed to see Bill Seager slowly cover it with the jack of hearts.

Bill then led the ace of clubs. I studied the two cards I had left, the king of spades and the queen of diamonds. Hoyle said to throw the queen of diamonds because that suit had already been played and the only diamond still out was the ten, while spades were yet unbroken. But in all deference to Hoyle, I'd sneaked a glance into Bill Seager's hand and seen the ten of diamonds there.

When Bill next led the ten of diamonds, Sniffy almost threw in the hand. But to his credit he didn't. And when I covered the ten with the queen of diamonds, he shouted, "Thank you, partner!" so loudly that Ruth swore she heard him at home.

Later I sat at the bar, buying rounds of beer and smoking my first cigar in years. Still beaming like a proud father, Sniffy turned to me with his own cigar and said, "A tie for first place ain't bad, is it, partner?"

"Not bad at all," I agreed.

Then he looked down at his beer and said quietly, "First time I ever won anything, Garth. Thanks for bailing this sad old man's ass out."

"You did most of the bailing," I said. "So keep your chin up."

"Dumb blind luck was all it was," he said, sinking deeper into his beer. "But like they say, every dog has his day."

"It was more than that, Sniffy," I said.

"How do you figure?" He laid his cigar in an ashtray as the bar began to empty.

"The way you played—for all the marbles, like there was no tomorrow, like every true champion plays. Even on that last hand, you weren't willing to settle for a tie, like I would have been. And had the cards fallen differently, and had you gone down, you still played it like a champ."

He raised his head to look around the bar. "Thanks, Garth," he said. "That means a little something extra coming from you." He drank the last of his beer, picked up his cigar, and slid off the bar stool. "But you can't tell me you wouldn't have gone for all the marbles either on that last hand. I know you too well for that."

I shrugged, then asked, "Where are you headed?"

"Home," he answered. "I don't want to close this place up, like I have too many times in the past."

"So you're going to leave that up to me?"

He clasped my shoulder on his way out. "It looks like it."

I sat drinking the rest of my beer while Hiram the bartender began to close up. Like all good bartenders, Hiram knew when to talk, when to listen, and when to leave you alone. That night I needed someone to talk to. "Hiram, doesn't Stub Timmons usually play euchre in here on Friday night?"

Hiram finished wiping the glass he held and put it away. "Come to think of it, he does. I can't even remember when he missed last."

"I wonder why he didn't show up," I thought out loud.

"Beats me. The only thing that Stub would rather do than play euchre is to count his money. Though sometimes I think even that's a toss-up."

"I didn't know Stub had that much money to count. The salvage business must be better than I thought."

Picking up another glass, Hiram began to dry it. "Better than I thought too," he said. "But he came in here late one night drunk as a skunk, carrying this wad of money, which he laid down on the bar and then began to count. Mostly twenty-dollar bills, I guess, with a few fifties and hundreds thrown in." He put the glass away and picked up another one. "When I wouldn't serve him, no matter how much money he waved in front of my nose, I thought he was going to jam the whole wad down my throat. Lucky for me Isabelle Glick came in right about that time and dragged him out of here."

"Isabelle Glick? Judge Glick's sister?" That was like telling me he'd seen Katharine Hepburn with Bill the cat. They didn't travel in the same social circles; they didn't even live on the same planet.

"Haven't you ever heard that misery loves company?" Hiram held the glass up to the light to examine it. "Stub Timmons and Isabelle Glick are about the two most miserable people I know. They used to be just sour on the world and everybody in it. Now they're just plain mean."

"Stub anyway," I said. "But I've always liked Isabelle."

"Then you're the only one in Oakalla," Hiram replied.

I drank the last swallow of my beer, which wasn't nearly as good as the first, paid Hiram what I owed him, plus a little extra, and left the bar. The stranger sat at the lunch counter where I'd left him at noon. He must have liked his privacy because he had the place to himself.

"Were you waiting on me?" I asked on my way out.

He didn't answer.

"Well, I'll be going then," I said.

"Where?" he asked. He had a low flat powerful voice that, like the pull of the tide, you couldn't ignore.

"Home."

"Good. Then I won't have to follow you."

"Why would you want to follow me?"

"My own reasons."

"Which are?" I persisted.

"My own reasons."

I shrugged and started to leave. Talking to him was like talking to the Sphinx, except the Sphinx was more amiable.

"Where I come from," he said, apparently to me, "a man would get shot for that little stunt you just pulled."

"What stunt is that?"

"Looking into another man's hand at cards."

That surprised me. I didn't think he'd been paying

all that much attention to me or anyone else in there. "Where I come from too," I said. "The trick is not to get caught."

"I'll remember that," he said.

Thinking that I'd scored a point with him, I was disappointed to see his dark-blue Chevy pickup follow me home. While I really didn't expect him to take me at my word, I did think that he'd keep his own word and not try to follow me.

Ruth waited for me in the living room. Though it was after midnight, she was still dressed. "What's the occasion?" I asked.

"No occasion. I just didn't feel like going to bed." She turned off the television, then sat back down in her chair. "How did you and Sniffy make out?" she asked.

"We tied for first."

"Tell me another one."

"It's true. We tied for first."

She shuffled through a stack of magazines for something to read but came up empty. "Who were you playing against, the Pee Wee Football League?"

"The regular crowd, minus Stub Timmons. He didn't show up tonight."

Setting aside the magazines, she turned her attention to me. "What's your point?"

"Today, when I wandered up to the north end to see Judge Glick, Stub Timmons intercepted me and made it clear that I wasn't welcome there. Then tonight I learned from Hiram that Stub Timmons and Isabelle Glick have some kind of thing going between them." Earlier that evening, over supper, I'd tried to tell Ruth how my day had gone, but once I mentioned Judge Glick, she had immediately changed the subject.

"You're drunk."

"No, but I'm close."

"Then Hiram's drunk."

"Hiram never drinks when he tends bar. I'm not sure he drinks when he doesn't tend bar."

She didn't believe me. "Then where did he ever get the idea that Stub Timmons and Isabelle Glick could ever have something going between them?"

I told her.

She still didn't want to believe me. "If Thorton knew that, it would kill him."

"*Thorton?*" I said in disbelief. "*Thorton?* Nobody calls Judge Glick *Thorton*. Not even his mother."

"You are drunk," she said, starting for bed.

"Then answer me this question. Why did *Thorton* kick Isabelle out of his house five years ago? Couldn't Stub Timmons have been the reason?"

She glared at me. According to Ruth's Rules of Order, some people were above reproach. Apparently Judge Thorton Glick and his sister, Isabelle, were among them.

"Then what was the reason?" I asked.

"I don't know what the reason was," she said. "And why is it any business of yours?"

"Because I think Judge Glick might be headed for trouble."

"Why?"

I leaned back in my chair and closed my eyes, but only momentarily. The room had started spinning. "I don't know why. Call it a gut feeling if you like. But I don't like the smell that's coming from that end of town."

"I'm going to bed," she said, dismissing me.

"Give him a call if you don't believe me."

"Give who a call?"

"*Thorton.*"

"Garth, have you lost all your senses? It's almost one A.M."

"So what? What's there to interrupt, besides his sleep?"

She started for the stairs.

"Then I'll call him."

That stopped her dead in her tracks. "No, you will not call him. You'll be looking for a new housekeeper if you do." From the sound of her voice, she meant it.

"Okay, I'll walk up there then."

"To do what?"

"If nothing else, make sure he got home okay."

"Home from where?" She came back into the living room.

"Wherever he went today."

"Start from the beginning," she said. "And don't leave anything out."

A few minutes later I slipped out the back door and walked north up the alley behind my house. I didn't see the dark-blue pickup following me, but I stopped every few feet just to make sure. White and on the wax, the moon lighted Fair Haven Road when the streetlights gave out. Streaked with high white clouds, the sky looked nearly empty of stars. Only the brightest were showing and those not as brightly as usual. With a sharp north wind in my face and the feel of snow in the air, I dreaded what might be on its way.

Judge Glick's gold Cadillac sat in his barn with the keys still in the ignition and the engine still warm. It smelled like rotten eggs inside it, the same smell that had been in Oakalla's water since the second day after the earthquake.

The back door of Judge Glick's house stood open. The house also smelled like rotten eggs inside. Then I saw the flicker of someone's flashlight.

"Judge Glick?" I called. "Is that you in there?" When he didn't answer, I went inside.

Unable to find a light switch, I took a couple steps while watching for the flashlight I'd seen earlier. When it didn't appear, something told me it wasn't going to

39

appear again as long as I was there. Something else told me that it wasn't Judge Glick who carried it.

Entering the kitchen, I searched for a light switch on both sides of the doorway. As I swept my hand along the cold smooth wall and lost my balance, I was reminded of my college days when I came home from a round of bars and tried to find the light with about the same results. Someone had either removed all the switches in the house or turned the house upside down in my absence; or so I thought until I discovered I was trying to turn on the light in our neighbor's gazebo.

I went into the parlor. Someone else was in there with me. I could smell him. He smelled like rotten eggs. Not knowing whether he was armed and unwilling to take the chance that he was, I tried to outwait him. Several minutes went by. Then I heard someone coming down the stairs. As I rose to intercept him, it didn't occur to me until it was too late that there might be two of them in the house.

Someone flattened me with his charge. He didn't intend to. I just happened to be between him and the parlor door. Momentarily without air and stunned from our collision, I lay on the floor gasping for breath, trying to blink away all the little sparkly things dancing before my eyes. The person who bowled me over went out the back door, and someone else went out the front door. And while I felt like a fool lying there on the floor of Judge Glick's parlor, listening to them leave without me, I couldn't do anything about it.

Finally I got up, wobbled around the room looking for a light switch, gave that up, and went looking for a lamp instead. Cradling it in my left arm to make sure it didn't get away, I turned on the Aladdin lamp that sat on the table in front of Judge Glick's east bay window. As I glanced around the room to see what might be missing, I was relieved to see that all of Judge Glick's rare books were still there. A couple had been pulled out and dropped on the floor, but when I put them back in place, I didn't see any empty spaces.

I called Rupert, who came at once. He too found nothing missing. "What about upstairs?" he asked.

"I haven't got that far yet."

"Then maybe we'd better take a look."

I followed him up a wide oak stairway to Judge Glick's bedroom, which sat in the northwest corner of the house and overlooked Stub Timmons' salvage yard. There we could smell a trace of hydrogen sulfide, like that of rotten eggs, but the smell wasn't nearly as strong as it was downstairs. Whoever had been upstairs didn't smell nearly as strongly of hydrogen sulfide as the one downstairs. Had it been smoke that we smelled instead, I would have guessed that the person upstairs had merely walked through some, while the person downstairs had been trapped inside a burning building.

"What do you think?" Rupert asked.

I stared at the gap in the bookshelf directly above Judge Glick's desk. "I think one of his books is missing."

"It looks like it, doesn't it," he agreed. "Anything else that you can see is missing?"

"No. But then I don't know what was here before."

He shoved a couple of books back in place. "You say his car is out in the barn?"

"Yes. The motor was still warm when I got here."

We went out to the barn. Taking the keys out of the ignition, Rupert opened the trunk of the Cadillac to look inside. Judge Glick wasn't there. We exchanged a look of relief. We both thought he might be.

"You have any idea at all where he went today?" Rupert asked, closing the trunk lid and handing me the keys.

"No. But he didn't go far." I opened the driver's side door to show him. "Danny changed his oil two months ago there at the Marathon. He's only gone fifty

miles since then. Even if most of it was today, he couldn't
have gone far."

"Far enough to get out of sight," Rupert pointed
out.

"You can do that in your backyard."

"Not in a gold Cadillac."

Rupert gave me a ride home where a light still
burned in the living room. "You talk to Rowena
Parker?" he asked before I got out of the car. In our
hurry to follow Judge Glick earlier that day, I'd forgotten to tell him about it.

"I talked to her and David both, but I didn't learn
much."

"You think they're up to something?" he asked, his
fingers quietly tapping the steering wheel.

"I don't know, Rupert. Those two are hard to read.
They always have been."

"David in particular, you mean."

"Rowena too. I got to know her a little better a few
months back, but I can't say I know her well." I
shrugged. "Some people are like that. They tell you only
what they think you want to hear."

"David doesn't tell me anything. He never did." He
rolled down the window to spit into the street. "I can't
figure it, Garth. I've got three sons. Robert, the oldest,
with next to all of the ability in the world, is living next
to a beach somewhere in Southern California with a girl
half his age. He hasn't done an honest day's work in the
last ten years and is not likely to again from what he
says. Jake, our middle son, who never had anything
come easy for him, and that includes walking and
talking, is a first-rate surgeon out in Baltimore." He
closed one eye and squinted at the streetlight. "Then
there's David with all of the ability in the world, who
hasn't turned one tap toward either making himself a
better person or this world a better place." He looked
my way. Hurt and shame showed in his eyes. "You tell

42

me, Garth, how two people like Elvira and me, who aren't perfect by any means, but still pull our own weight at home and on the job, how we can raise a son like David, or even Robert for that matter, who no more resembles us and our way of thinking and doing things than I do the man in the moon. Where did we go wrong? That's what I can't figure out."

"Do you want an answer?"

"*Yes*, I want an answer. If you have one."

"I don't."

He allowed himself a rare smile, or as close as he ever came to one. "I figured you probably didn't."

"People are for the most part what they are," I said. "And there's very little that you or I can do to change them."

"I was thinking about when they were kids," he replied. "It's too late now for me to do anything about it."

"I wouldn't know about kids," I said. "My son didn't live long enough for me to find out."

"If he had lived, how do you figure he might have turned out?" Rupert said. "Like you?"

"I don't know, Rupert. I'd like to think he'd have some of my values, or at least those I try to live by. But I'm enough of a realist to know that there's no way to guarantee that. Even if there were, maybe my values wouldn't have worked for him. Sometimes they don't— father to son. I'd hate to think I would have made him miserable, trying to be me."

Rupert sighed. "That's sort of the way I figure it too. But it's hard to stand by and watch your son make a wreck out of his life." He shook his head in frustration. "Especially when you know what it's doing to his mother."

"I hear you," I said. "But I still don't have any answers."

He put the car into gear. "When you do, let me know."

I handed him a slip of paper with a 1955 Montana license plate number on it. "When you get a chance, have Clarkie run this through his computer for me."

Taking the car out of gear, he glanced at the slip of paper. "I already have," he said, handing it back to me. "The pickup belongs to a Blackfoot Indian named Tom Two-Feathers. He died in 1967."

I glanced across the street to where the pickup was parked. "Why doesn't that surprise me," I said. My eyes still on the pickup, I asked, "So what do you plan to do about him?"

Rupert nodded toward the pickup. "Him being the one in that pickup over there, the one that's got everybody in Oakalla buffaloed, including me?" he asked.

"And me," I added.

"I'm not sure what there is to do about him. He hasn't broken any laws that I know of."

"What about driving an unlicensed vehicle?"

Rupert turned to spit out the window. "Even that might get a little tricky, since the same rules that apply to us don't always apply to Indians, especially those still on a reservation." He rolled up the window. "But I think I could press the point if I wanted to."

"Why don't you want to?"

"I'd kind of like to know what he's doing here first, wouldn't you?"

"In the worst way. But I haven't noticed that he talks about himself much."

He put his car into gear. "Keep after him, Garth. If anybody can get to him, you can."

I looked at him. "You're kidding, of course."

"Of course." But he didn't appear to be kidding.

I opened the door to let myself out. "That's what I thought."

Ruth waited for me inside. From all appearances

she hadn't made that first move toward bed. "Well?" she said.

I told her what all had happened. When I finished, she sat back in her chair with a stony look on her face. She was still sitting there when I went to bed a few minutes later.

5

The third blue day in a row greeted me as I stepped outside my front door the next morning. Unlike the previous two days, there was no wind blowing, no wispy white clouds to dull the sun and stripe the sky. A perfect March Saturday lay before me, begging me not to waste it indoors. Glancing from the sky to the ghost-green trees in front of my house to the old blue pickup parked across the street, I promised I wouldn't.

Rupert picked me up in his patrol car just as the pickup pulled away from the curb and started uptown. We drove to Judge Glick's house to see if he'd returned in the night. He hadn't.

"What do you think?" Rupert asked as we sat in Judge Glick's drive with the motor running.

"I think we ought to go to Jimmy Parker's."

"Why? I've been there twice already. Nobody's home."

"Did you go inside?" I asked.

"No. The door was locked. Besides, I didn't see the point of it."

"I think we ought to go inside," I said.

"Why? I'll need a reason if we do that."

"Isn't the fact that he and little Jimmy are missing enough reason?"

"Not if we go by the book. Since we don't even know for sure they're missing," he added.

"When has that stopped you before?" I asked.

"It's always stopped me before," he said. "You're the one it's never stopped."

"Are you saying I'm above the law?"

He gave me a strange look. I couldn't tell whether he was angry or not. "I'm saying that it's easier to do my job your way than it is to do it mine. You'd find that out if you'd put on this badge for a week."

"I don't want to put on your badge for a week, or even for a day," I said. "I just want to find Jimmy Parker and his son. Don't you?"

He put the car in reverse and backed out onto Fair Haven Road. I knew then that he was angry with me, but he wouldn't say why.

"Where are we headed?" I asked.

When he didn't answer, I guessed we were headed to Jimmy Parker's house.

But somebody else had beat us there. When we got to Jimmy's small two-story frame house in the near west end of town, we discovered the front door open and the contents of every shelf and drawer dumped on the floor. Thinking I heard someone leaving, I went around to the back of the house and saw David Roberts walking up the alley toward town. He seemed in no hurry, as though he didn't care if anyone saw him or not.

"See anything?" Rupert asked on my return to the house.

"No. It must've been my imagination."

He glanced sharply at me. "Mine too. I could've sworn I just saw my youngest son in the alley behind the house."

"Leave David to me," I said. "I'll talk to him later."

Rupert's face looked drawn as if in pain, and he

47

appeared to be short of breath, as he had been a couple of days earlier. "Better you than me," he said.

"Are you all right?" I asked.

He didn't answer right away.

"Rupert?"

"I'm fine, Garth," he insisted. "Just give me a minute to collect my thoughts."

Several minutes passed. While Rupert sat on the sofa "collecting his thoughts," I took a brief tour on my own. I went from the living room into the small sunlit dining room that was the coziest room in the house, through the kitchen to Jimmy's bedroom and back out again, then down wooden stairs to a half basement, which was about as dank and dreary as a basement could be.

"For a handyman," I said to Rupert, brushing the cobwebs off of me, "Jimmy sure doesn't do much homework."

"I think every tool he owns he carries in that El Camino of his," Rupert said. "And as far as handymen go, he wouldn't be the first I'd call if I got in a pinch."

"Me either," I agreed. Then I asked, "How are your thoughts?"

"Collected," he answered, rising from the couch.

At the top of the stairs we found young Jimmy's bedroom, a small pair of silver-and-red pajamas lying on the bed, a sad-eyed stuffed dog sitting on the bed beside them, a couple of small, paint-skinned metal cars that had apparently crashed on more than one occasion, and a yellow plastic plane, obviously broken.

"It doesn't look like the little fellow has much to play with," Rupert said, picking up the plastic toy and trying to piece it back together.

"Not by today's standards," I said, folding the pajamas and picking up the dog to look at it.

"What are you planning to do with that?" Rupert asked.

I set the dog back down again. "Nothing, I guess."

"We're a fine pair, aren't we?" he said, kneeling to right one of the toy cars.

"A fine pair," I answered. I stared at the metal door that led into the next room beyond Jimmy's. "I wonder what's in there," I said.

Rupert gave the tires a spin and set the car back down. "There's only one way to find out." But when he tried to open it, he discovered that the door was locked. No amount of pressure would budge it either.

"It looks like we've reached a dead end," I said. "Unless you have a suggestion."

"That we leave well enough alone for now," Rupert replied. "That's my suggestion."

"Back to that again," I said.

"Back to that again," he answered.

We went downstairs where the mess looked even worse than before. Whoever had trashed Jimmy's house had done a thorough job of it, leaving nothing untouched.

"What do you figure they were after?" Rupert asked, picking up a stack of photographs that had been dumped on the living room floor.

"I have a guess," I said. "If you remember, Jimmy Parker stopped by Judge Glick's house on his way out of town last Saturday. Maybe it was to borrow something."

Rupert had found a photograph that captured his attention. Glancing over his shoulder, I saw that it was an early photograph of the Jimmy Parker family, when Jimmy and Rowena were still together, and little Jimmy was about a year old. It looked very much like the last photograph ever taken of the Garth Ryland family— even down to the underlying sadness hidden just beneath their smiles.

"You think it was to borrow a rare book?" Rupert asked, laying the photographs aside.

"I think it's possible. It looks like one of Judge

Glick's rare books is missing. His house has been ransacked and now Jimmy Parker's has. So you can take it from there."

While Rupert questioned Jimmy Parker's neighbors, I went looking for David Roberts. I found him in a booth at the Corner Bar and Grill drinking coffee. The brooding hulk of the stranger sat at his usual place at the counter, commanding the room. Except for Bernice the co-owner, we three were the only ones in there.

I took a seat at the booth across from David and ordered a cup of coffee. "I wouldn't if I were you," David said. "It tastes like crap."

"Is that right, Tom Two-Feathers?" I asked the stranger. "How is the coffee this morning?"

He turned on his seat at the counter to look at me. He wore the same clothes, hat, and belt that he had the first time I saw him, the same dour look. "You don't waste any time, do you?" he said.

"Time is money, someone said."

"But you're not in it for the money," he replied, then turned away to drink his coffee.

"What was that all about?" David asked.

Still puzzled by the stranger's last remark, I took a moment to answer. "Apparently an inside joke," I finally said.

"Then you know him?" David said, his eyes on the stranger.

"As well as I do you."

David laughed and didn't say anything more.

Bernice brought my coffee. I added cream and sugar and took a taste of it. David was right. It tasted worse even than our coffee at home."

"I warned you," David said.

"So you did," I answered.

He waited for me to continue. When I didn't, he

said, "I suppose you're wondering what I was doing in Jimmy Parker's house this morning."

"Your father and I both are."

"Leave my old man out of it, okay?" he said. "If you want any answers from me."

I took another drink of my coffee and tried to act calmer than I felt. I hated to hear any son refer to his father as "my old man," particularly David Roberts. "Whatever suits you, suits me," I said.

The stranger grunted loudly enough for us to hear, but said nothing. I could tell, however, that he had read my thoughts.

"You have something to say?" David asked the stranger.

"Not to you," the stranger replied without even bothering to look at him.

That exchange seemed to unnerve David, who wasn't used to being ignored. "Go to hell," David said.

"Thanks, but I've been there," the stranger answered in the same low rumble.

"We already have a bill on the floor," I said to David. "You were about to tell me why you went to Jimmy Parker's house."

His eyes still on the stranger, David said, "I went to Jimmy Parker's house because Rowena asked me to. She said that he might have come back in the night and just not bothered to tell us; or bothered to answer his phone whenever she called. But when I got there, I found both doors wide open and the place was a mess, so I left." Turning to me, he said. "You can ask Rowena if you don't believe me. I hear you two are pretty good at asking each other questions."

Though he wore his old familiar smile, his voice seemed to have a slight edge to it. I wondered what I might learn about David Roberts if I pushed hard enough, besides the fact that he was sleeping with Rowena and referred to Rupert as his "old man."

"That's not all we were good at," I said.

David's next move took us both by surprise. He wanted to hit me so badly that he tried to stand up in the booth, but only succeeded in spilling his coffee all over the table. Embarrassed for the first time in my memory, he slid out of the booth and exited the Corner Bar and Grill without paying for his coffee.

The stranger watched him go, then said with gruff appraisal, "It looks like you hit a nerve."

"It looks like we both did," I said, feeling my arms still trembling in anger.

I paid for David's coffee and my own, then stopped beside the stranger on my way out. "What did you mean when you said I'm not in it for the money?" I asked.

"Just that."

"Not in what for the money?" I persisted. "Because I can guarantee you that I like it just as well as the next man. Maybe more. It's just that I never seem to have much."

He shrugged. "But you always have enough, don't you? That's what I meant."

"Enough for what?" I asked, still puzzled.

"You figure it out," he answered. "I've got my own problems."

I still hadn't figured it out when Rupert found me walking north on Fair Haven Road and gave me a ride as far as Isabelle Glick's house. "What did you learn from David?" he asked.

I told him what David had told me.

"Do you think he's telling the truth?"

"He might be," I replied. "He might not be. You know David."

"Yes," he said. "I know David." He spat into Isabelle Glick's gravel drive. "About as well as I know that rock over there."

"What did Jimmy Parker's neighbors have to say?" I asked.

"What's that, Garth?" He was somewhere else, probably still thinking about David.

"Jimmy Parker's neighbors, what did they have to say about whoever broke into his house?"

"Most of them didn't have anything to say because they hadn't seen or heard anything out of the ordinary. But Sadie Jenkins, who keeps a pretty good eye on things in that part of town, said she saw both a white pickup and a dark-colored older pickup in the neighborhood recently. The older pickup might have been blue, purple, or black. She couldn't be sure."

"Recently? Does that mean last night?" Because Tom Two-Feathers' pickup had been parked across from my house when I went to bed the night before and then again when I got up that morning.

"More like real early this morning," he said. "She saw the dark pickup first, parked along the street there in front of her house. Then the white pickup came along and parked in the alley behind her house. She said it was the first time she'd seen the white pickup in the neighborhood. But the dark one's been there regular the past few mornings when she's gotten up."

"What time does Sadie get up anyway?" I asked.

"Before you or me," he answered. "But that's not the point. The point is what is Tom Two-Feathers, or whatever his name is, doing in the neighborhood? And even more to the point, what does he want with Jimmy Parker?" He looked at me hopefully. "Any chance he'll tell us?"

I smiled. "Percentagewise, I'd say we'd stand a better chance of asking his pickup."

"That's what I figured."

"Which leaves Stub Timmons' white pickup still unaccounted for," I said.

"We don't know it's Stub's," he corrected me.

"Who else in town drives a white pickup?" I asked. "Right off the top of your head?"

He had to think about it and still couldn't come up with anyone. "I see what you mean," he said.

"So do you want to talk to Stub or should I?" I asked.

"I'm not sure either one of us should," he answered. "I've had my eye on Stub Timmons for a long time. I know he's up to something, but I can't figure out just what. And that wad of money he was flashing around town only confirms the fact."

"How did you know about that?"

He gave me a forgiving look. "Garth, there's not much that goes on around this town that I don't know about." He nodded in the direction of Isabelle Glick's house. "Particularly late at night."

"So what do you think we should do?"

"Do whatever you think's best," he answered. "Just don't crowd Stub too hard or you'll scare him off from whatever it is he's up to."

I opened the door and started to get out. "Wish me luck," I said.

"I'll be down at the pump house if you need me."

"Another water sample for the State Board of Health?"

"Yes," he said without enthusiasm.

"Is our water getting worse?"

"Not so you'd notice, but it's not getting any better either." He shook his head wearily. "I don't know, Garth. For the good of all concerned, I'm trying to keep this under my hat, but I feel like I'm sitting on top of a powder keg. One wrong move and the whole thing's going to blow up in my face."

I could almost feel his tension. I also knew why he was at cross-purposes with himself over the water. Why on the one hand he felt obligated to warn the people of Oakalla of their possible danger, and yet on the other hand he wanted to keep it quiet. Along with the other problems that the knowing might cause, there was also

54

the very real possibility that the state or federal government might step in and take over. Neither Rupert nor I wanted that. We both felt strongly that we in Oakalla could best take care of ourselves.

"Hang in there. We'll get to the bottom of it yet," I said.

"Soon, I hope. Soon."

He drove away. I watched him go with an uneasy feeling in my guts. For the first time since I'd known him, Rupert Roberts didn't like being sheriff.

Isabelle Glick lived in an old two-story frame house that had once belonged to Hermine Good, who died without money, heirs, or debts, leaving her property at the mercy of the elements until the town of Oakalla figured out what to do with it. It was gray and paintless, plastic covering its windows and rags stuffed in the holes in its siding. Claiming to be Hermine's long-lost great-grand-nephew, Wilmer Wiemer had somehow gotten the rights to the house and then rented it to Isabelle Glick when her brother had put her out of his house and forever barred her from its door again. An eyesore, even when Hermine Good lived there, the house had gone steadily downhill until it seemed that only Isabelle Glick's unbending will held it together.

Stepping lightly around the holes in the porch, I knocked on the storm door, which rattled loudly and threatened to fall off its hinges. I knocked again. When no one answered, I opened the storm door and tapped on the glass inside.

Isabelle Glick had a way of looking down at you no matter what her circumstances. Nearly six feet tall with winter-white skin and pale turquoise eyes that seemed to burn right on the edge of madness, she wore a mink stole, a straight, floor-length red dress, red half-moon earrings, a smear of red lipstick on her mouth, and red rouge on her white cheeks. Orangish red threaded with gray, her hair was held in place by a pair of ivory combs,

55

while her brows arched in two thin brown lines above her eyes. At first glance you'd never know that Isabelle Glick was anything but the dowager she appeared to be.

"What do *you* want?" she asked me.

Shortly after I moved to Oakalla and started the *Oakalla Reporter*, someone wrote an anonymous letter to me as editor that I refused to print. The letter, which among other things claimed that Judge Glick was a bumbling fool and that Oakalla was being used as a hazardous waste dump by a person or persons un-named, had a venom to it that I found objectionable, so when no one ever stepped forward to claim it, I threw it away. Apparently Isabelle Glick had never forgiven me for that.

"I wondered if I might come in a moment," I said.

"Why?" she demanded.

"Because I'm afraid I'll fall through the porch if I stand here much longer."

"Take it up with Wilmer Wiemer. It's his property, not mine."

"I'd rather take it up with you."

She studied me a moment. I didn't know why I always felt uncomfortable under her gaze, but guessed it had something to do with her eyes, which seemed to see right into my soul. Then she threw open the door and I followed her into her living room, which was bare of all furnishings except for two straight-backed wooden chairs and a portrait painting hung on one wall in a heavy walnut frame. The man in the portrait wore a black judge's robe and the stern certain look of a man for whom judgment came easily. I could tell from the portrait where Isabelle Glick got her turquoise eyes. I could also tell where she got her strength.

"My father," she said in explanation.

"I guessed as much."

"Not a better man ever walked this earth," she said reverently. "Nor a better judge."

"I guessed that too."

She sat down in one of the chairs where she crossed her legs and lit a cigarette. I sat down in the other one. In the time it took for her to smoke her cigarette, neither one of us said anything. I rubbed my hands together to warm them. It was cold in there out of the sunlight.

"So talk," she said. "If that's what you came for."

Isabelle Glick had been an accountant for nearly as long as her brother Thorton had been a judge. Tough, shrewd, and thoroughly honest, she had earned a reputation that made her the most feared business-woman in Oakalla. Isabelle Glick could seemingly make or break you with one small calculation, and though by all accounts she used her powers wisely and judiciously to the benefit of all concerned, she never earned much friendship. Like the iron-faced schoolmarms who made scholars out of generations of ignorant farm boys, Isabelle Glick kept us all at arm's length partly to keep her eye on us and partly to demand deferential treat-ment from us. Machiavelli said it was better to be feared than to be loved. Isabelle Glick seemed to agree.

"Did you know your brother Thorton was missing?" I asked. "That he hasn't been seen or heard from since yesterday morning?"

She uncrossed, then crossed her legs again, lighting another cigarette. "My brother and I have not commu-nicated in the past five years," she said coldly. "So whatever happens to him is of no concern to me."

"Not even if he might be in danger?"

She took a long drag on her cigarette, as the smoke leaked slowly from her nose. "Not even if he were dead."

We stared across the bare room at each other. I met her gaze without giving much ground, not an easy thing for me to do with Isabelle Glick. "Then I guess I'm wasting your time," I said.

"It appears so," she replied, but made no move to dismiss me.

"One of your brother's rare books seems to be missing, the one he kept in the middle of the first shelf right above his desk. You wouldn't happen to know which one that is, would you?" I asked.

Her eyes narrowed. Then she laughed. "Good God, no! I don't know which one that is. And furthermore, I don't care."

"What about Jimmy Parker?" I said. "Do you have any idea why he might have stopped by to see your brother last Saturday?"

"No idea whatsoever," she answered.

"Is it true that Jimmy used to do odd jobs for your brother before your brother's stroke?"

"Odd jobs indeed," she said. "What he did was certainly odd and precious little of that."

"Do you mind explaining yourself?"

She shrugged as if it meant nothing to her. "Most of the time that Jimmy Parker spent in our house was spent in Thorton's library, pouring through Thorton's old books, instead of fixing whatever it was that needed fixing. But whenever I mentioned it to Thorton, he would say to leave the boy alone, and that somebody at least appreciated his books as much as he did."

"Do you know what there was in them that Jimmy Parker found so interesting?" I asked.

If she did, she wasn't about to tell me. "You can ask him that," she said. "The next time you see him."

"Jimmy Parker and his son are missing, just like your brother. Or didn't you know that?"

She just stared at me like a cat measuring a mouse.

"Sorry to have bothered you." I rose to leave.

"You and my precious brother," she said. "You both think you can save us all from ourselves. Well, you can't."

"You didn't feel that way eight years ago," I said.

That got her attention. "Explain yourself, please." It was a command, not a request.

"The letter you wrote me about your brother. And what certain unnamed people were doing to the land around Oakalla."

"What about my brother?" she said.

"You called him a bumbling fool among other things. You said he wasn't fit to be a judge, or anything else that required any judgment on his part. Then you went on to say that someone was dumping hazardous waste in and around Oakalla under his very nose, but that he was too blind to see it." When she didn't answer, I said, "Or have I misquoted you? After all, it's been almost eight years."

"I never wrote that letter," she said quietly.

"Then who did?" Whether she had written it or not, she didn't like to be reminded of it.

"I don't know." She pointed her cigarette at me in anger. "But had you printed it, had you somehow found the courage and listened to it and not your wallet, or whatever it is you listened to in that case, perhaps we wouldn't be having this conversation right now." She looked around the bare bleak room as the wind made the plastic at the curtainless window bulge. "And perhaps I wouldn't be living in exile in this dump."

"Exile from what?"

"My brother's last judgment," she answered, rising from the chair and mashing her cigarette underfoot. "Now there's the door. Use it."

"If we find your brother, should I let you know?"

"Do whatever you like," she said wearily. "Nothing matters anymore anyway."

Stub Timmons didn't seem pleased to see me. We stood just inside his building with the door closed behind us. The long-haired white cat still lay outside in the puddle where he'd thrown it. The smell of grime and axle grease clung to the cool thick air of the building like an oily fog. I thought I caught another scent as well—the smell of rotten eggs.

"What are you doing back again?" Stub asked uneasily. "You were just up here yesterday."

"Judge Glick is missing. I wondered if you knew where he might have gone."

He looked around for something to do and found a fender that he threw into a large pile of assorted junk. "How am I to know where that old fool went to. It ain't up to me to keep track of him." Picking up a hubcap, he threw that into the pile. "Now, as you can see, I'm busy."

I studied his concrete-block building, which had double overhead doors on the front of it, a small single-paned window on the south wall, a clogged floor drain that smelled like sewer gas, several scattered piles of junk, and the look of poverty. The girlie calendar that hung on the wall just inside the door was spotted with grease, while the gray time clock beneath it whirred and ticked and drew attention to itself. I wondered why Stub needed a time clock anyway, unless to keep track of his own hours.

"What are you looking at?" he asked. "Ain't you ever seen a naked woman before?"

"Your time clock," I answered. "I've never seen one at a junkyard before."

"It ain't for me," he said brusquely. "It's for somebody else."

"I didn't know anybody else worked here."

"They don't. But they used to."

"I see," I replied, even though I didn't.

"No, you don't see," he said, taking a step toward me. "Amos Stryker used to work here for me years ago. The laziest cheatinest sonofabitch I ever came across. I had to buy the time clock to keep him honest. Otherwise, he would have stole me blind, which he very nearly did anyway." He knelt to pick up a drive shaft. "That's what it's here for."

When the drive shaft slipped out of his grasp and fell at my feet, I got the message. "If you hear anything from Judge Glick, be sure to let me know," I said on my way out. "My number's in the book."

He stood with his huge arms crossed and a scowl on his face and said nothing.

Once outside, I stopped to pick up the cat by its tail and took him along with me. "Hey! Where are you going with Tom?" Stub yelled at me.

"To get him out of the cold."

"It's my cat, goddamn you! Leave him be!"

I didn't try to answer him. I just kept on going and left it up to Stub to stop me. He took a couple steps my way, but that was as far as he got before he wheeled around and went back inside.

In Judge Glick's barn I found a shovel that I used to bury Tom under an apple tree. I didn't know what Tom thought about it, but I felt a lot better. Then I climbed the stairs to Judge Glick's bedroom and stared out his west window at Stub Timmons' salvage yard where one row of junked cars followed another like hills of potatoes. Standing there in the quiet, surrounded by shelves of rare books and other relics from the past, I felt that time could stop, the world end, and I might never know it for weeks if I never left that room. Its peace, pure and undistracted, was deceiving, however. For a stone's throw away lay the crumpled remains of parts that had hummed, wheels that had sung, engines that had roared. Struck by the paradox, the abrupt unbending silence of all graveyards, I turned to Judge Glick's desk where the space from the missing volume gaped. I doubted that I would ever return Judge Glick to that room, but somehow, by finding the missing volume, I might return big and little Jimmy Parker to Oakalla, and in the process help return Oakalla to normal.

6

"Are you sure this is legal?" Edgar Shoemaker asked.

He and I stood outside the metal door in Jimmy Parker's upstairs. Edgar carried his cutting torch. I carried a small tank of acetylene which I had set on the floor of young Jimmy's bedroom to give my arms a rest.

Glancing out Jimmy's south window, I saw the sun was finally up. But it was about the only thing up except for Edgar and me on that cold, quiet March morning. "I don't know if it's legal or not," I said. "But it's necessary."

"This could land us in jail, you know that," Edgar warned as he lit his torch.

"So what else is new. That never stopped us before."

"I swear, Garth, you're going to make an old man out of me yet," he said just before pulling down his welding mask.

While Edgar worked on the door, I kept one eye on Center Street and the other on the lookout for stray sparks. Jimmy's sad-eyed stuffed dog watched the whole affair with a half smile as if he halfway approved of our actions, but wasn't quite sure what his master would think. I assured him that what we were doing was best for all concerned.

"Done," Edgar said, shutting off his torch. "But you'd better give it some time to cool before you try to go in there."

"Are you going in there with me?"

"Might as well," he said, lifting his mask and lighting a cigar. "I can't see much anyway."

We waited while the door cooled. I could hear nearby church bells ringing for someone's sunrise service. I wondered why they were having a service so early until I remembered it was Palm Sunday.

"Well," I said. "Do you think it's cool enough?"

"You might give it a try."

Wearing the gloves I wore into the house, I pushed on the metal door and felt it give as a cold wave of air rolled out at me. A moment later I stepped inside. Edgar followed.

Indian artifacts that included beads, arrowheads, jewelry, pottery, tools, knives, spears, bows and arrows, and many other things that I could only guess about had been randomly thrown into wooden boxes piled one on top of another until there was hardly room to walk among them. Two skulls sat side by side in a wicker basket on top of a wooden ceremonial mask of some kind. One of the skulls appeared to be that of an adult, the other of a child. I knew by their shapes that they belonged to an earlier age of man, but just how much early I didn't know. Early enough, I guessed, to qualify for museum pieces. But that could be said for almost everything in there.

I set the basket of skulls aside and held the wooden mask to my face. "What do you think?" I asked Edgar.

But the mask was wasted on him. Unable to see me clearly at that distance, he couldn't see how hideous I looked. "I think we'd better get the hell out of here and tell somebody." He picked up a hammered silver bracelet and held it up close to his one good eye. "This stuff must be worth a fortune."

63

I laid the mask down and set the basket of skulls back on top of it. As I did, one of the skulls rolled my way. I caught it just in time. "At least a fortune," I agreed.

Laying down the bracelet, he picked up a stone war axe that still had the handle attached. "Where do you suppose Jimmy got all of this stuff?" he asked.

"Only he knows. But one thing's for sure, he's made a science of it."

One wall of the room, twelve feet by at least seven feet, was completely filled with books on Indian lore. Some of the older rarer editions could have come from Judge Glick's collection, perhaps purchased from Judge Glick by Jimmy over the years, or given as payment for his handiwork. But looking through them, I didn't find any one title that jumped out at me, or gave me cause to believe that anyone but a purist would be interested in possessing it.

"Just what are you looking for, Garth?" Edgar asked.

"The book that seems to be missing from Judge Glick's bedroom. The one that sat front and center above his desk."

"It's not the one on Wisconsin folklore, is it?" Edgar asked.

I tried to remember if I'd seen such a book there. "I don't know, Edgar. How do you happen to know about it?"

"The Judge gave it to me for safekeeping a few years back. He said that of all the books in his collection, it was the most valuable, and he wanted to make sure it fell into the right hands if anything ever happened to him."

"The right hands meaning who, his sister Isabelle?"

Edgar shook his head. "Nope. Her name wasn't mentioned. A couple of familiar names were, though. Sheriff Roberts was one of them. Ruth was the other."

"Ruth Krammes, my housekeeper?" I found that hard to believe.

"One and the same."

"I'll have to ask her about that when I get home. But if Judge Glick gave you the book for safekeeping, then how did it end up back at his house?" I said.

Edgar puffed on his cigar a couple of times but couldn't get it to go. Instead he laid it down and picked up a clay pipe to puff on. "You remember that spell I had with my lungs a while back, when I wasn't quite sure I was going to make it? Well, I made up my mind right then that I'd better get the book back to the Judge in case I died before he did. No telling where it might end up once my nieces and nephews got ahold of it." Taking the clay pipe out of his mouth, he eyed it with distaste before putting it back in its box. "Or whoever would get the first crack at it."

"Was Judge Glick glad to see it again?" I asked.

"Hard to say, Garth. He'd had that stroke of his in the meantime. I'm not even sure he recognized the book, or at least the value he once put on it."

"Do you remember what was in it?"

"Nope. I never even opened it. I figured that would be too much like snooping."

"Would you recognize it if you saw it again?"

"I might." He shrugged. "Then again I might not."

Before we sealed the door on Jimmy Parker's room, I searched through the books on Indian lore, but didn't find any on the folklore of Wisconsin. Though I did find something that intrigued me on the opposite wall, which was a large topographic map of eastern Adams County that had been made by piecing together four different quadrangles. Also included in the map were bordering sections of the adjoining counties.

Small X's had been penciled in to mark different spots throughout the county. I called Edgar over there. "What do you make of it?" I asked.

He leaned close until he nearly touched the map. "They look like they might be digging sites to me," he said.

"You might be right." I pointed to the one farthest away, right on the border between Adams and Red Lake counties. "How far would you say it is from there to Oakalla? Maybe fifty miles round trip?"

Edgar traced the route with his finger. "Closer to forty, I'd say."

Remembering that Judge Glick's Cadillac had only gone fifty miles since its last oil change, I said, "That means Judge Glick could have driven out to any one of them and back and still had some miles to spare."

"At least it means his Cadillac could have," Edgar pointed out. "I don't recall seeing the Judge around lately."

I took a last look around the room. I felt there the way I sometimes felt in the basements of museums when the lights were dim and nobody else was around. On those occasions the past seemed to come to life around me, and I spent more of my time looking over my shoulder for mummies than I did at the exhibits themselves. Along with the artifacts that filled the room, Jimmy Parker had dug up graves, belongings, bones, and culture, and claimed them for his own. Maybe it didn't bother him, having them there in his house, but it would have bothered me.

After Edgar welded the door closed, I drove us to the north end of town, parked Jessie, the brown Chevy Sedan that I'd inherited from Grandmother Ryland, in front of Edgar's shop, and walked to Judge Glick's house. The feeling of uneasiness that had come over me at Jimmy Parker's followed me there as I searched upstairs and down without finding the book on Wisconsin folklore. Then on the way home I noticed that the sky was less blue than earlier that morning. A thin white layer of clouds had overspread it. The air too seemed

66

sharper than it had earlier. It blew from the north-northeast and felt as if it came straight from the heart of Lake Superior.

Ruth sat at the kitchen table with a cup of instant coffee in front of her and a scowl on her face. Apparently I'd disrupted her privacy because she seemed to resent my being there. "I thought you and Edgar had plans for this morning," she said.

"We did. We're done with them."

"Then what are you doing back here?"

I glanced around for something to eat and quickly grabbed a box of Grapenuts before Ruth could get up from the table and start making something that I didn't have time to eat. "The last time I looked," I said, "I lived here."

She let that pass without comment.

"But don't worry," I continued. "I'm just passing through. I'll be out of your way before you know it."

"You're not in my way," she said.

"You couldn't prove it by me."

"I was just listening to the church bells." She rose from the table, took the box of Grapenuts out of my hand, and set it back in the cabinet. "That's all." She took an iron skillet out from under the stove, put some bacon into the skillet, and began beating eggs for what I hoped was French toast.

I got down my coffee cup, put some instant coffee in it, and added boiling water. Though Ruth claimed the water was getting better, it still smelled bad to me. "You'll never guess what we found at Jimmy Parker's," I said.

"Probably not." She wasn't in the mood to guess.

I told her.

It didn't seem to bother her like it did me. "Can he get away with keeping all that stuff?" she asked.

"He has so far."

"I mean legally."

"I don't know. But I don't want to talk to Rupert about it."

"Why not?"

I added half-and-half and sugar to my coffee. "Because what Edgar and I did is called breaking and entering. Rupert wouldn't approve."

"Why? He's looked the other way before when you did something out of line."

I tasted the coffee. No matter what Ruth said, it didn't taste any better to me. "I can't pin it down exactly, but something's really getting to him. And even though he's asked for my help, now is not the time to test him."

Ruth began turning the bacon. "You might be right about that," she said. "You remember you asked me to find out what I could about him. Well, I tried, but nobody seemed to know why he was so down on things, only that he was. So I went right to the horse's mouth herself and asked Elvira."

"And?" I said, waiting for her to turn the last piece of bacon, which was giving her a hard time.

"Rupert's been having chest pains. But she can't get him to go see the doctor about it."

"Damn," I said.

"So what are you going to do about Rupert now that you know what his problem is?" she asked.

"I don't know," I answered. "It might help if you'd tell me what you know about a book on Wisconsin folklore that Judge Glick gave to Edgar Shoemaker a while back for safekeeping."

She turned to face me. "What are you talking about?"

"Judge Glick gave Edgar a book with instructions that if anything ever happened to him, the book should fall to either you or Rupert. I just wondered if you'd ever seen the book, or could tell me what was in it."

She turned back to the stove without answering.

"Ruth?" I was going to prod her if I had to.

"You said you were just passing through," she said. "Where are you going from here?"

"The Barrens. Now, are you going to answer my question, or not?"

"What are you going to the Barrens for?"

"Because I think that's where Judge Glick might have gone after he left here last Tuesday."

"Do you think it's a good idea to go over there by yourself?"

"Damn it, Ruth," I said angrily. "Quit changing the subject. What do you know about a book on Wisconsin folklore?"

"Nothing."

"Then why would Judge Glick leave instructions with Edgar for it to fall to you if anything happened to him?"

"It wasn't just me," she was quick to point out. "I believe you mentioned Rupert in there somewhere too." She dropped a piece of bread into the egg batter, then put it into the skillet where she sprinkled it with cinnamon and powdered sugar.

"Rupert's the sheriff," I said. "If it had any legal ramifications, it should naturally fall to him. But what I want to know is where are you in the order of things?"

"What do you mean, where am I in the order of things?"

"Were you and Judge Glick lovers at one time?"

It suddenly got very still in the room. "Garth Ryland, I'll pretend I didn't hear that."

I got up and dumped my coffee into the sink. "I won't pretend I didn't ask it."

"Where are you going?" she asked.

"I told you. To the Barrens."

"Not without breakfast, you aren't."

"Are you going to tell me what went on between you and Judge Glick?"

"No, it's none of your business."

"Then I'm going without breakfast." I was leaving when I looked out the window and saw a dark-blue 1955 Chevy pickup with a camper on the back pull up and park across the street. "Damn," I said.

"Something wrong?" Ruth asked, looking like the cat that ate the canary.

"I need a favor."

She set the platter of bacon and French toast on the table. "We can talk about it over breakfast."

7

So named because it was the least populated—and acre for acre the most desolate—part of Adams County, the Barrens lay about twenty miles east-northeast of Oakalla and included the small town of Lee, Halsmer Airport, and a small section of Red Lake County. Neither unusually stark nor particularly rugged in its topography, the Barrens had come to be called that because throughout its history, nothing, from farms to settlements to industries, seemed to prosper there for very long. The town of Lee, once a railroad center, was nearly a ghost town. Halsmer Airport had a hangar and a runway, but the weeds grew high on the runway by late summer, and in winter the airport was abandoned altogether.

Those hardscrabble souls that had survived in the Barrens beyond just a few years had done so mainly in isolation, living simply and frugally, and taking whatever the Barrens gave them in return for their perseverance. Small scattered shacks dotted the Barrens, like the miners shacks that once dotted the Colorado foothills, but most were deserted and had been for years. So even if you survived in the Barrens long enough to put down roots, that was no guarantee that you would continue to survive there.

No one knew exactly why the Barrens had proved so inhospitable. One school of thought claimed that the soil was the problem. It was too thin and sandy and too vulnerable to erosion. Others, including Hattie Peeler and Big Charlie Smith, both full-blooded Chippewa, said that the porous limestone beneath the soil would not support the weight of civilization, that under pressure to produce, it cracked and buckled, fell into caves and sinkholes, swallowed earth, man, and his dreams.

I glanced in the rearview mirror of Ruth's Volkswagen but didn't see anyone following me. After breakfast, Ruth had backed Jessie out of the garage, turned around, then driven south down the alley behind our house toward town. I watched from the living room as the 1955 Chevy pickup pulled away from the curb and followed her. Then I'd left the house on the run and driven north on Fair Haven Road in Ruth's Volkswagen. At Haggerty Lane I turned east, all the while keeping an eye on the rearview mirror to make sure our ruse had worked. When I determined that it had, I relaxed and enjoyed the ride.

I would have enjoyed it more had the sun been brighter, the sky not so milky white. When the sun went under the clouds for good, I saw that the sky wasn't white at all, but a tattletale gray that had only appeared white as long as the sun was out.

The farthest *X* on Jimmy Parker's map took me to a part of the Barrens that I'd never visited before. A winding gravel road led me up a gentle grade and then down into a narrow forested valley where the road ended at a burned-out homesite. A second, steeper, narrower road twisted its way up the next ridge, but unwilling to put Ruth's Volkswagen and my nerves to the test, I left the car beside the burned-out homesite and began to climb the ridge on foot.

I hoped to find a house in the next valley and maybe somebody at home, but I wasn't encouraged by either the ruts in the road or the burned-out homesite I'd left behind. Thirty-five years ago, according to the topographical map I carried, a building of some kind had sat in the next valley. I figured that if I reached the building and came up empty, as I had at all of the other digging sites, I'd turn around and go home.

At the top of the ridge a drop of sleet hit my nose. In the valley below, Jimmy Parker's El Camino sat beside a small log cabin that took me only a couple of minutes to reach.

Weather-beaten and windowless, the cabin was covered with a rusty tin roof and a thick layer of leaves and debris. A pitcher pump stood on the porch, and the shell of a privy stood several yards behind the cabin.

I knocked on the door of the cabin. When no one answered, I went inside in the hope that there might be someone about. Dark and cool, the cabin had four nearly square walls and the flavor of wood smoke. An ancient pot-bellied stove sat in the center of the cabin, and a rusty stovepipe led from it to the roof. But there were no lights of any kind that I could see, not even a kerosene lantern.

Something moved in the far corner of the cabin. It sounded too large for a mouse. "Who's in here?" I asked.

"No one" came the answer a moment later. It sounded like a young boy.

"Jimmy, is that you?"

"No."

"Then who are you?"

"No one," he repeated.

"And you're sure you're not here?"

"Yes," he answered, though he was sounding less sure of himself as we went on.

"Fair enough," I said. "If you don't want to be here,

73

I won't make you be. So I'll just leave now and let you alone."

I hadn't taken more than a few steps toward the door when he rushed out of the corner toward me. With barely time to brace myself before he got there, I caught him and held on as he buried himself in my arms. Terrified, he clung to me with all his five-year-old might, as if I were his last hope on earth.

"Don't leave me," he pleaded.

"I won't, Jimmy," I said, tousling his hair and taking a firmer hold. "I promise I won't."

A few minutes later Jimmy and I stood at the cabin door, watching it rain. Overhead it lightly tapped the tin roof, while in the distance it fell like fog, glazing the trees with ice.

"We have to go," I said to Jimmy, knowing that we had at the most an hour to get out of there before the roads iced over and became impassable.

"Not without Daddy," he said, reluctantly tearing loose from me.

"We don't know where Daddy is," I replied.

"Yes, we do," he insisted. Pursing his lower lip, he intended to stand firm to the end.

"Then where is he?"

He pointed to the east, which was in the direction of the X on Jimmy Parker's map. "There."

"We'll come back for him tomorrow."

He shook his head, as tears came into his eyes.

"Okay," I said. "We'll go look for him. But if we don't find him soon, we're going to have to leave."

"Why?" Now that he had company, he seemed almost content to stay there.

"Because your mother misses you and wants you home."

"No, she doesn't," he said with a scowl.

"Of course she does," I argued.

He folded his arms. "No, she doesn't."

74

I smiled at him. Though I'd tried to find the resemblance, he didn't look at all like Jimmy Parker to me. Jimmy Parker was slight and fair with a round face, big blue eyes, and pointed ears that always made me think of an elf. And his movements were quick and sharp, and elfin in their unpredictability, as were his moods. He could do a minor job of building or home repair cheaper, faster, and at least as well as anyone else in Oakalla, so he always had all the work he wanted. But the larger jobs, those that required planning or led to complications, seemed to frustrate him at every turn. So in the end he usually jerry-built them and went on to something else. Sometimes they held up. Often they didn't. But being the sprite that he was, Jimmy Parker dodged criticism as easily as he did his creditors, and no matter what you might think about his work, you still liked him, and hired him again whenever you had the chance.

Young Jimmy on the other hand reminded me of a small Rupert Roberts. He had Rupert's large ears and somber face, Rupert's basset eyes and his deliberate movements and expressions, as though life was always serious, and nothing he ever did was haphazard or accidental. Gaunt like Rupert, particularly after his stay in the cabin, he could also dig in his heels when he wanted his way and defy you to change his mind. With that in mind, I at least had some idea of what to expect from him.

"Why doesn't your mother miss you?" I asked.

"Because I don't know," he answered. "But she doesn't."

"I know somebody that misses you," I said, grasping for straws.

He stuck out his chin, looking as stern as one can at five. "Who?"

"Just think about it a minute." I stalled for time as the rain came down.

Then he sighed. "I know someone," he said sadly.
"Who?"
"Mickey."
"Who's Mickey?"
"My dog."

I remembered the sad-eyed dog that sat in the corner of Jimmy's bedroom. "Of course, Mickey. I just talked to him this morning. He said he misses you."

"No, you didn't," he said. "You made that up."

I reached into my pocket and took out a handful of change. "Bet you a quarter I didn't."

Reaching into his own pocket, he discovered it was empty. But that didn't daunt him any. "What does Mickey look like?" he asked.

I told him.

"Where does he sleep?"

"In your bed. But you left him on the floor."

"Didn't either," he said. "Daddy put him there. He said I could bring him along the next time."

"Well, whatever the case, Mickey misses you and wants you home."

He had to think it over. "Okay," he said, taking my hand. "I'll go home."

"Without your daddy?" I asked hopefully.

He shook his head. "No. You promised we'd look for him."

We stepped out into the rain and walked east along the floor of the valley. I wore jeans, hiking boots, my woolly jean jacket with the collar turned up, and buck-skin gloves. Jimmy wore a lined nylon jacket, jeans, tennis shoes, and my blue stocking cap, which he had pulled down over his eyes so that only his nose showed. Hand in hand, we climbed the hill at the far end of the valley. There, about half way up, we discovered the mouth of a cave.

"Did your daddy go in here?" I asked Jimmy.

"I don't know."

"Do you want to go in here?" I hoped he didn't, because I didn't like caves, closets, or any other closed-in places.

"Maybe," he said bravely. "For a little bit."

With Jimmy clutching my back pockets and hanging on for dear life, I took a deep breath and began to crawl through the narrow limestone chute that led into the cave. At the first tight squeeze I fully intended to stop and turn around because I knew I couldn't make myself go any farther. Jimmy didn't much care for the cave either. His grip got tighter and tighter and his arms got stiffer and stiffer until I was dragging him along behind me like a two-bottom plow.

I heard him whimper. "What's the matter?" I asked.

"I'm scared."

"So am I. Do you want to go back?"

"No."

Instead of narrowing, the cave gradually began to open up until I no longer needed to crawl, but could walk bent over, and then at full height. I stopped. I didn't know how far we'd gone, and I could no longer stretch out my arms and feel the cave wall on each side. Without a light, it would be too easy to get lost in there.

"Jimmy!" I yelled. "Jimmy Parker, are you in here?" My voice reverberated off the walls, traveled on and on without returning. That bothered me. The cave seemed much larger than I first thought.

"We'd better go back," I said to Jimmy. "Is that okay with you?"

"Okay with me," he said solemnly.

I had to smile. He sounded just like Rupert. "Would you rather that you lead and I follow?" I asked. "Or the other way around?"

"The other way around."

"Okay," I said, turning him around. "Here we go."

It was still raining when we cleared the cave. I put

Jimmy on my shoulders because we could travel faster that way and started across country toward Ruth's Volkswagen. Twice I slipped on the ice underfoot and nearly went down. The third time I landed flat on my back and lay there stunned, while Jimmy crawled out from under me and lay with his head in my lap without saying a word. I put my arms around him and held him until he stopped shaking, then continued.

Ruth's Volkswagen couldn't climb the icy hill out of the valley. It tried its best, but even with the motor in the back and the full weight of my hopes and prayers upon it, the best it could do was to get us in sight of the top before it stopped and started sliding backward. Finally I had to give up and park it at the bottom of the hill where we started. Otherwise, I might lose control of the situation altogether and end up in the bottom of a ravine.

Had I been alone, I would have walked out of the Barrens for as far as it took me to find a ride home. But I couldn't leave Jimmy there by himself, and I couldn't very well walk the five miles or so I needed to go with him on my shoulders.

"We have to go back to the cabin, Jimmy," I said.

"No, I want to go home. I want to see Mickey." He began to cry.

"We can't go home, Jimmy. It's too slick."

"Then I want to stay here."

I tried to imagine what it was to be five years old again. In his eyes we had probably come a long way from the cabin in the next valley north. To return to it would seem a terrible journey that would take us even farther from home.

"We can't stay here, Jimmy," I said. "It's too cramped and there's nothing to eat."

"I don't care," he said. "I don't like that other place."

"I don't much like it either," I agreed. "But maybe it won't be so bad with both of us there."

"That's what Daddy said." He wiped his eyes with the back of his hand. "But he left me there all alone."

"For how long did he leave you there alone? Do you remember, Jimmy?"

"Long" was all he knew.

"Well, I won't leave you there alone. And we'll start for home the first thing in the morning."

He looked up at me with those solemn brown eyes of his, wanting to be reassured. "Promise?"

I raised the appropriate fingers on my right hand. "Scout's honor."

"You're not a scout," he said.

"No, but I once was." I didn't think it was necessary to tell him that I wasn't a very good scout by scout standards.

Back at the cabin I took inventory to see what we would need to last the night, and perhaps the next day or two if it came to that. Foodwise we were okay. Jimmy Parker had brought in beef jerky and trail mix and there was still some of that left, along with the two Snickers I carried in my coat pocket. We also had a couple of Cokes left from the case he'd bought at the Marathon, and the pitcher pump outside in case we needed water. I worried most about staying warm, since there was no wood in the cabin and no axe that I could find. I did find a couple of blankets, though, and wrapped Jimmy in one while I started to go look for wood.

"I want to go with you," he had said stubbornly, shaking off the blanket.

"I'm not going that far," I answered. "Besides, it's still raining."

"I don't care. I want to go with you."

"Well, you can't. You'll just have to trust me to come back."

"That's what Daddy said," he pouted.

"Well, I'm not your daddy," I said on my way out.

I found a dead cedar and began breaking off its branches. When I had an armful, I carried them to the porch of the cabin where I knocked the ice off of them before I went inside. As Jimmy watched the pile of cedar grow and grow, his spirits rose. So did mine when I found two kitchen matches in my coat pocket that were left over from the last time I burned the trash at home.

But before I tried to start the fire, I first made sure that the stovepipe was open all the way to the roof, then searched until I found a couple of old newspapers stuffed in a chink in the cabin wall. I put the papers in the stove and was ready to strike my first match when I saw a lump in the back of the stove that didn't look like either coal or ashes. I reached into the stove and pulled it out. *Folklore of Wisconsin*, its title read.

Fascinated, Jimmy watched me light the fire, then slowly feed it cedar twigs until I had a cheery blaze going. But soon his eyelids began to droop, and the next thing I knew he lay asleep on the floor beside me.

As I opened *Folklore of Wisconsin*, I discovered an envelope that had apparently been used as a bookmark. Someone had made notes on the back of the envelope in a small unsteady script that I had a hard time reading. I could make out days of the week, times of the day, and a few of the corresponding names, but little else. I recognized a couple of the names as belonging to small industries near Oakalla, but I couldn't understand, for example, what Greenwall Manufacturing was doing at three P.M. on a Wednesday, or why it was important enough for someone to make a note of it. So I folded the envelope, put it into my shirt pocket for safekeeping, and began to read the "Lost Tribe of Oakalla," which was the first chapter in *Folklore of Wisconsin*.

"Many years ago, before the white man came with his thunderstick and took the land for his own, there lived on the central plain of Wisconsin the tribe, Oakalla. . . ."

A poor tribe of hunters and fishermen, their range had shrunk over the years until the Oakalla were forced into their last remaining valley where they would have perished except for their one great hunter and warrior—Matatomah, the "Horrible One," as he was known to his tribesmen and enemies alike, who was "as foul as his brothers were fair."

Hunting alone in the barren hills, he found game where there was no game to be found. Walking barefoot among the rocks with only a willow branch in hand, he found water where no one else could. Guarding the village at night while his tribesmen slept, he kept wild animals and enemies alike away.

"Then one spring day a deep rumbling shook the valley, opened a hole in the rocks, and dared anyone to enter. . . ." No Oakalla would enter the cave, however, not even Matatomah, who knew through a vision that he would one day die there. But a drought followed later that summer and Matatomah finally was forced to go into the cave to find water in order to save his people.

"Courage, he told himself. He must have courage. For a man marked by the gods to be so hideous in appearance that even old grandmothers ran from the sight of him must have been blessed with a great task or duty. Otherwise, the gods would seem callous and capricious by making a mockery out of this their greatest creation, man. . . ."

Matatomah found more than he bargained for. There in the cave he found a great river that not only quenched his thirst but also gave him strength untold. Though reluctant at first to taste the water because they feared a trick, Matatomah's tribesmen soon discovered its amazing powers and began to fight among themselves for the rights to it. To stop the fighting and so preserve the water for all of his people and all of the generations of Oakalla to come, Matatomah was forced to set up residence in the cave where he doled out the water himself, and he became, instead of the Oakalla's greatest warrior, its most steadfast servant.

For generations the Oakalla prospered, regained through battle all of the land taken from them in the past, and then expanded it to include nearly all of Wisconsin. Meanwhile, Matatomah grew rich as the keeper of the water. But he also became blind.

Toward the end of his life he wished that he had not rejected the gift of the beautiful maiden whom his people had once offered him, and who, after she had borne him a son, would have been free to leave the cave to marry someone of her own choosing. For a son was all that Matatomah required to continue his legacy, and his son's sons, and their grandsons after that. Without that faithful guardian, "Matatomah feared for his people even more than he feared for his beloved river. . . ."

Then a second earthquake came, which proved every bit as powerful as the first. It sealed the entrance to the cave and buried Matatomah somewhere below. And though the Oakalla searched night and day for months on end, they never did find the entrance again.

"Two generations later the last of the Oakalla fell, it is said, on the very spot where Matatomah once knelt and begged his people to drink. It is also said that Matatomah's river is still flowing far beneath the earth, and sometimes, when he thinks about his lost people, it becomes brackish, which is the salt of Matatomah's tears."

I closed the book and listened to the rain upon the tin roof of the cabin. The fire had burned down, leaving the cabin chill. Little Jimmy began to stir under his blankets. After tucking him in and assuring him that all was well, I rebuilt the fire and waited for morning.

8

Sometime in the night the rain stopped. The stillness that followed was one of the deepest in my memory, encased as it was in a shell of ice as hard and tight as an oyster's.

I heard the footfalls long before they ever reached the cabin. Crunch, crunch, crunch, they came out of the night toward us. Sitting up on the floor, I put one hand on Jimmy and reached for a stick of cedar with the other. Bam! Something hit the door of the cabin, shook the rafters, and caused dirt to rain down upon us. Bam! The second blow awakened Jimmy, who stared at me in wide-eyed terror. I put my finger to my lips for silence, and he responded by tunneling under the blanket as far as he could go.

Bam! The third blow nearly caved the door in. I rose and stood with the stick of cedar in my hand, wishing it were the size of a baseball bat. In the following moments I could hear someone breathing heavily just outside the door and was tempted to open the door to see what might happen. But I was also afraid of who it might be and what he might do to Jimmy and me once he got inside.

So I waited for the fourth blow, which never came.

Instead, I heard footfalls leaving, and they crunched through the ice until I heard them no more. Waiting until I thought it was safe, then hearing a limb snap and waiting a couple of minutes more, I opened the door of the cabin and looked outside. By the light of the nearly full moon, which hung in a pale halo over the glazed branches of the trees, I saw a solitary figure climb the hill to the east and disappear into what seemed to be the mouth of the cave. Then the wind brought a familiar smell to me, the smell of rotten eggs.

Meanwhile, Jimmy had crawled out from under the blankets to stand beside me. He carried a chunk of wood nearly as big as he was and looked as though he meant to use it. I smiled and tousled his hair. "Let's go back inside," I said.

"Who was that?" Jimmy asked, as I used our remaining wood to stoke the fire.

"I don't know, Jimmy," I answered.

"What did he want?"

"It sounded like he wanted in."

Jimmy drew closer to me. "Was he trying to get us?"

"I don't think so. He probably didn't even know we were in here." Though he could no doubt smell the smoke from the fire.

"Where did he come from?"

"I think from the cave."

"Daddy's in the cave," Jimmy said fearfully.

"We don't know that for sure, Jimmy."

"Then where is he?"

"I don't know, Jimmy. But once I get you home, I'll get help and come back looking for him."

"Can we go home now?"

I lay down on the floor and covered us both with the blankets. "As soon as it's daylight."

At dawn I rose and left Jimmy asleep while I went outside. Bent low to the ground by the weight of the ice, the trees already sparkled in morning's first light. Sun dogs and rainbows were everywhere, and crystal garlands hung from the cedars like Christmas tinsel. Once I'd taken it all in, I went back inside.

For breakfast Jimmy and I had beef jerky and Coke. When the ashes finally cooled, I scooped them from the stove, piled them in the blankets, knotted the blankets, and left. Jimmy held on to me with one hand and carried *Folklore of Wisconsin* in the other; I carried the knotted blankets Santa-like over my right shoulder. For each two steps forward, we seemed to slide one step back, and we had to stop frequently to rest and to shift our loads back and forth. At the rim of the valley we made our last stop. Glancing down at the trees, iced and afire with sunlight, I felt as though we had just escaped from Oz.

Ruth's Volkswagen didn't want to start, but finally it did. After I got it going, I had Jimmy keep his foot on the accelerator as I chipped the ice off the windshield and the side windows. I stopped scraping once, to glance behind me at the rim of the valley we'd just left. It seemed as though someone was there, watching us. Though I couldn't see him, I felt his presence. I also felt that the sooner we left, the better.

I then took a handful of ashes at a time and spread them under the tires of the Volkswagen and on up the hill as far as I could before I ran out. At the most I needed ten more feet's worth of ashes to reach the crest of the hill and do the job right. There was probably that much ash left in the stove back at the cabin, but I didn't go back for it.

"Ready?" I asked Jimmy.

He looked up at me trustingly. "Ready."

"Then hold on tight."

I put the Volkswagen in reverse and eased it back a foot or so to get a good grip on the ashes. Shifting to first with no intention of ever shifting to second, I pointed the Volkswagen up the hill, let up on the clutch, and took off. Once we began to roll, I eased down on the accelerator in the hope of building as much speed as we could before we ran out of ashes. The Volkswagen began to whine in protest. It had never seen thirty in first gear before, and with Ruth at the wheel, was not likely to again. We hit bare ice and I almost lost control when the rear end slid around and started us into a spin. Easing up on the gas to straighten us out again, I lost momentum and felt the hill sliding out from under us. Inches from the top, the Volkswagen seemed to stop altogether. Jimmy and I both leaned forward and rocked as the engine revved to a high-pitched scream and the tires began to smoke.

Almost there, but not quite over the hump, the Volkswagen began to side sideways again, and I knew we'd come up short. But rather than let it end there, which would have been the smart and safe thing to do, I left the road and began to drive parallel to the crest of the hill, looking for an opening. I found one in the form of a small notch where the hill leveled out before rising sharply again. With no idea of what was on the other side, I aimed for the notch, crowded the Volkswagen through it, and headed straight down the hill.

I wanted to angle for the road and intersect it from alongside, but the Volkswagen had other ideas. We shot across the road at the first bend, kept on going through a meadow, and luckily met the road again at the next bend, where I finally had enough control to keep the Volkswagen in the roadway. But we weren't out of the Barrens yet. We had to strain for every mile of the way until at last we reached a road that had been salted.

I leaned back to rest my head on the seat. Drenched with sweat and so tired that I trembled, I actually wondered if Jimmy could drive us on to Oakalla.

"Are we there yet?" Jimmy asked, trying to peer over the dash.

86

"No," I said with a smile. "But we're on the downhill slide."

Jimmy gave me an anxious look.

"That means we're almost there," I assured him.

Clarkie met us on Fair Haven Road on our way into Oakalla. I knew there was something wrong before he ever put on his red light to stop us. Had Rupert had anything to say about it, he would never have let Clarkie drive out of town on the morning after an ice storm.

"I was just coming to look for you," Clarkie said. "Sheriff Roberts is in the hospital. Elvira took him there early this morning."

"What's wrong with him?"

"They think it's his heart, but they won't know for sure until they run some more tests on him."

"How is he?"

Clarkie didn't know what to tell me. "I don't know, Garth. As well as can be expected, I guess."

"Have you seen him?"

"No. They won't let anybody in to see him until they find out for sure just what's going on."

I put the Volkswagen in gear. "Thanks, Clarkie. I'll get to the hospital as soon as I can."

Clarkie leaned out of his window and smiled. "And who do you have in there with you?"

"Jimmy Parker," Jimmy answered for himself.

"I can take him home," Clarkie said to me. "If you'd like to go on to the hospital."

I looked at Jimmy. He didn't look like he cared much for that idea. "Thanks, Clarkie. But Jimmy and I have come this far together. We'll go the rest of the way."

"Any word on his dad?" Clarkie asked.

"Yes and no. I'll fill you in later."

"What did that man want?" Jimmy asked when we were nearly to the Marathon.

"A friend of mine is sick. They had to take him to the hospital."

"Real sick?" He looked concerned.

I forced a smile. "I don't know yet, Jimmy."

Before I took him home, I stopped at his dad's house to pick up Mickey, his stuffed dog. Entering the house, I felt like an intruder, as I had at first in the farmhouse after Grandmother Ryland died. The feeling stayed with me all the way up to Jimmy's room and back down again. But as I walked away from the house, I left it behind.

Rowena Parker tried to hug Jimmy when we arrived, but he pulled away and ran on into the house past David Roberts, who stood in the doorway of the living room. While Rowena ran after Jimmy, I asked David, "How's your dad?"

"I wouldn't know."

"Haven't you been to see him?"

"No. Haven't you?" he said sharply. "I would have thought you'd have been the first one there."

"I've been out of town looking for Jimmy."

David Roberts didn't try to hide his bitterness. "And for that I'm supposed to thank you." Then he closed the living room door on me before I ever had a chance to answer.

I drove to the hospital and went into the waiting room where Elvira Roberts sat by herself in one corner on a red plastic chair with a stack of knitting in her lap. Short, pert, and plump, Elvira Roberts hadn't changed in the eight years I'd known her. She still looked ageless, somewhere between sixteen and sixty, with a dimple on her chin, a twinkle in her eye, and a reputation for making the best pumpkin pies in Oakalla. I loved Elvira Roberts for the same reasons that I once loved Grandmother Ryland—for her goodness, her good nature, and all the little things she did to spoil me.

As soon as I came in, Elvira set aside her knitting

and rushed halfway across the waiting room to hug me. "How are you doing?" I asked.

"A lot better than I was a few minutes ago. Dr. Lind just came in to tell me that he didn't think there was any damage to Rupert's heart itself, but he wanted to keep him here a couple more days for tests just to make sure."

She took a handkerchief out of her purse and blew her nose while I put a blue plastic chair beside her red one. "Then did he actually have a heart attack?" I asked.

"The same as one, the way the doctor explained it to me. He couldn't get enough blood to his heart through his veins, and that's what caused the chest pains." She blew her nose again and put her handkerchief away. "It's stress, the doctor thinks. From everything he knows so far, he doesn't see how it can be anything else."

"So what does Dr. Lind suggest?"

"Rest for now. He thinks Rupert should spend a couple more days here in the hospital and then at least a week at home before he goes back to work."

"What does Rupert say about that?"

She gave me a worried smile. "You know what he says about that. I'm having a hard enough time keeping him in here now."

"I'll talk to him," I said. Then I returned her worried smile. "For the good it'll do."

She patted me on the shoulder. "It can't do any harm."

Rupert was sitting up in bed looking out the window when I entered his room. He looked about the same as he had the day before. Perhaps he was a little paler, a little less sure of himself, but all in all he didn't look too bad. Though I would never get used to the sight of him in a hospital gown.

"Better than the last time you saw me in here," he said, reading my thoughts. "It's all on the inside this time."

"How are you feeling?" I asked, pulling up a chair beside his bed.

He frowned. "Like I'm wasting the taxpayers' money lying here. The way the doctor tells it, it's all in my head."

"That's not exactly the way I heard it," I said.

"Well, that's the way it is," he said stubbornly.

An uncomfortable silence followed. Usually we didn't have any trouble speaking our minds to each other. That day we did.

"I found little Jimmy Parker," I said to break the drought.

If he was happy to hear the news, Rupert did a good job of hiding it. "Where?" he asked.

"An old cabin out in the Barrens."

"Was Jimmy's dad there too?"

"No, but his El Camino was."

"You have any idea where his dad is?"

I thought of the cave. The thought of going in there again actually turned my stomach. "Some, though I'm not too anxious to go looking for him."

"Why's that?"

"He's likely in a cave there in the Barrens. You know how I am about caves and other closed-in places."

Rupert nodded. He knew how I was. He felt the same way about heights. "What's Jimmy Parker doing in a cave in the Barrens?"

"Looking for Indian treasure, I think," I said. "I came across this old book in the cabin where I found little Jimmy. It has quite a story in it that I want you to read sometime. There might be enough truth to it in Jimmy's eyes to warrant going into the cave to see what he might find."

Rupert studied me. "I can see why he might have gone into the cave," he said. "Jimmy's always doing some kind of harebrained stunt like that. But what I want to know is why he never came out again. Or how you

90

ended up in the Barrens looking for him in the first place."

"I got lucky, that's all," I said. "I played a hunch and it panned out."

"What hunch was that?" he wanted to know. "You went into that room after all, didn't you" he said. "After I told you not to."

"I had to, Rupert. I didn't have a choice."

"You had a choice," he chastised me. "You just chose not to exercise it."

"Damn it," I said. "Would you rather I left little Jimmy Parker out in the Barrens to freeze to death?"

His eyes began to wander, and he suddenly looked very tired. "That's not it, Garth."

"Sorry. I think I've overstayed my visit."

His face seemed to soften, as he lay back on his pillow and closed his eyes. "How is the little fellow?" he asked.

"What little fellow?" I wondered if he was dreaming.

"Jimmy Parker. You said you found him."

"He's fine," I said. "A little worse for wear and tear, but not much. He's a tough little nut." Just like his grandfather, I almost added.

"That's good," he mumbled. Then he offered his hand and I shook it. But his grip didn't have its usual strength. "Keep me informed."

"I plan to," I said.

His eyes opened momentarily. "And make sure Clarkie takes a water sample every day and gets it to the State Board of Health."

"I'll be sure to." Then I started to say something else about the water and the crazy thought I had, but changed my mind. His eyes had closed again.

"What was that?" he asked.

"I didn't say anything."

He rolled over on his side. "My mistake. I thought you did."

Oakalla looked no less dazzling than the Barrens had, following the ice storm. Every bush and every tree wore a brilliant white sheen; every power line sagged under the weight of the ice, cracked and crackled in the wind; every eave and every roof sparkled in the bright noonday sun and made even the plainest house look grand.

After calling Ruth to tell her I was home, I ate lunch at the Corner Bar and Grill, then began making and taking calls and working on the *Oakalla Reporter*. I'd only been away from my office for a couple of days, and I usually didn't work Sunday anyway, but since I'd missed Monday morning and all the things I usually did then, it seemed I was already a week behind.

Several hours later I looked up from my desk to see that it was dark outside. The streetlights along Gas Line Road had already come on, illuminating the trees, which still wore their icy coats, and reflecting off of the patches of ice still on the road. Nowhere did I see a headlight or a taillight. Nowhere did I see anyone walking Gas Line Road. I leaned back in my chair and thought about all the things I still had left to do before Friday's deadline. On top of that, Oakalla's water was still bad and Jimmy Parker and Judge Glick were still missing. I closed my eyes, wishing I could sleep.

Ruth ignored me when I walked in the back door at home and sat down at the kitchen table. She stood at the stove fixing supper with a determination that usually meant she was angry about something.

"What's wrong?" I asked.

She wouldn't look at me. "You know darn good and well what's wrong. It doesn't take a genius to figure it out."

"If you're mad because I didn't call you till today, I couldn't. We didn't have a phone where I was."

"Guess again."

I closed my eyes and rubbed the back of my neck, trying to let some of the tension go. I wished I didn't have anything to do after supper. "People have been calling here wondering where I was, Edna Pyle in particular?"

She stirred whatever it was she was fixing and what smelled to me like vegetable soup. "True, but it's not that either."

I straightened and stretched my arms. "Then I give up," I said.

She waved her stir spoon at me. "What always happens when you make me drive that rattletrap car of yours?"

I knew then what was the matter. Ruth and Jessie mixed about like oil and water. "Where did Jessie quit on you?" I asked.

"The far south end of town," she said. "About as far south as you can get and still be in Oakalla. Which is, if I remember right, where you sent me." She waited to make her next point clear. "And Jessie didn't quit on me either. I ran out of gas."

"Oh," I said.

"That's not the worst of it. Who do you think it was that first came to my rescue?"

"Rupert."

"You're not even close."

Then I had a sobering thought. "Tom Two-Feathers."

"In the flesh. He walked up to me, took a long look inside your car, and said, without a smile I might add, 'That's one for you.' Then he got into that old blue pickup of his and drove away."

"Where did he go?"

"What do I care where he went!" she said. "I had to walk six blocks in my housecoat to the Marathon, past the Methodist church on a Sunday morning, just be-

93

cause you were too lazy to put gas in your car the last time you drove it."

"I wasn't too lazy," I said in my defense. "I just didn't have the time."

"Well, you've got plenty of time to go chasing here and there around the countryside for who knows what. And plenty of time to spend the night away from home while I sit here in the dark because the ice storm knocked the power out." She turned back to the stove to stir the soup. "Then when you do call, you say, 'I'm home, Ruth.' Just like you've been out on a lark somewhere, and not stranded in the most godforsaken part of Adams County on the worst night of the year." She stood with her feet spread and her hands clenched into fists. "Does it ever occur to you what might go on here while you're away?"

"No," I said. "But I'm learning."

She dumped a spoonful of soup back into the pot without ever tasting it. "As well you should."

"I'm sorry, Ruth," I replied. "I didn't mean to worry you, and I'm sorry about you and Jessie. But I couldn't have Tom Two-Feathers, or whoever he is, following me. And if I had driven Jessie, I might still be out there in the Barrens right now."

"Then I think it's time for you to get a new car."

"New cars still run out of gas," I pointed out. "In this case it wasn't Jessie's fault, but mine."

Ruth glanced at the ceiling. "You heard him, Lord. You'd better mark that down because it's a first." She added more pepper to the vegetable soup and tasted it. "Now, what did you learn for all of our troubles?"

I told her. When I finished, she said, "But you didn't find Judge Glick?"

"No. Or Jimmy Parker either."

"Jimmy Parker I can live without," she said quietly, as if she didn't want to discuss it further.

"But I did bring you something to read," I said,

laying the book, *Folklore of Wisconsin,* at her place at the table. Then I marked the "Lost Tribe of Oakalla" with the envelope I'd found inside the book. "This story in particular."

Ruth didn't miss many tricks. "Interesting bookmark," she said as she picked it up and examined it. "Where did you get it?"

"It was in the book. I think the book belongs to Judge Glick. But I'm not sure about the bookmark."

"It's his too," she said with certainty. "I'd recognize his writing anywhere."

9

Late that night it started to snow, and it continued to snow throughout the next day. A heavy wet snow that fell straight down upon an already thick layer of ice, it broke tree branches, snapped power lines, made the streets of Oakalla and the roads of Adams County temporarily impassible, and generally put everything on hold. Slogging to and from work, to the Corner Bar and Grill for lunch and back to my office again, I was thankful for the respite, the chance to put my own house in order, and relieved that I didn't have to go back into the cave looking for Jimmy Parker.

On Wednesday it began to thaw under a warm March sun and a clear blue sky. When I was a kid, nothing had ever smelled so good to me as the first real thaw of spring after all the long and stuffy months indoors. Thaw meant I could go fishing once again, or ride my bike around town, or play baseball, or collect butterflies. But best of all, it meant no more school. No longer would I have to answer a bell, or stand in line for lunch, or stop where the road met the schoolyard. Soon I could go wherever and whenever I chose. Each day wouldn't have a box around it, and each adventure a time limit. Thaw meant that I could live my life right then and there, instead of waiting for someone's permission. Thaw meant that I was free.

On Thursday I visited Rupert at his home. He wore a robe over his pajamas and a pair of leather slippers that looked as old as Ruth's housecoat. He also wore the look of a man still at odds with himself. When I asked him how he felt, he said, "Better."

"Good," I said. "When does that mean you can go back to work?"

"Whenever I feel like it," he said without enthusiasm.

"On a reduced schedule," Elvira added from the kitchen.

"What does that mean?" I asked Rupert.

I thought I saw pain in his eyes, and what appeared to be resignation. "It means I'm getting old, Garth," he said. "That I'm not the man I used to be."

"That's not true, Rupert Roberts!" Elvira came to the doorway of the kitchen. "What it means is that you've been working too hard and Dr. Lind wants you to take it easy for a while."

He turned to look at her. His face showed his anger and frustration. "It means I'm getting old," he repeated. "That the job's too much for me."

Elvira threw up her hands and retreated into the kitchen. "Talk some sense into him, Garth. I can't seem to."

"She's right, you know," I said to Rupert, even though he wasn't in the mood to hear it. "You have been under a lot of pressure lately. You've even said so yourself."

"I always handled it before," he said gloomily. "You tell me what the difference is now." He looked down at his hands, checkered and weathered from years of working out of doors. "Except my age."

"Circumstances," I said.

"Hell, Garth, I went through a world war! Don't talk to me about circumstances."

"You were nineteen years old then."

"Which proves my point." Though he seemed to take no satisfaction in proving it.

"Okay," I admitted. "Your age does have something to do with it. But so does mine. I can't do the things I used to do at nineteen either, or even the things I used to do at thirty. That still doesn't mean I can't handle my job any more than it means you can't handle yours. Just give yourself some time. Things will even out. They always do."

"And what happens the next time Oakalla's water goes bad? Or somebody turns up missing?" He held up a bottle of nitroglycerin pills. "Do I reach for one of these?"

"If you have to," I said. "But I don't think you will."

"Why not?" He clutched the bottle as if he wanted to throw it out the window. "What'll be the difference between then and now?"

I rose to leave. "You will. You won't let this get you down any more than you've let things get you down in the past."

"And I think that's a bunch of hogwash," he said angrily. "A lot of things got me down in the past. I just didn't let them keep me there."

"Same difference," I said, then left.

On Thursday at noon I walked to the Corner Bar and Grill for lunch. With the temperature nearly fifty outside, Gas Line Road a river of melted ice and snow, and the *Oakalla Reporter* well on its way to completion, I didn't mind jumping over puddles and dodging the cars that came splashing down the road toward me. My good mood lasted all the way to the Corner Bar and Grill, right up until that moment when I walked inside and saw the stranger sitting alone at the counter. He hadn't been in the Corner Bar and Grill all week, and all week

98

the Corner Bar and Grill had been its old lunchtime self again, filled with loud talk and laughter. Immediately I saw and heard the difference that his presence made. Like the proverbial wet blanket, he put a damper on everyone's good time.

Instead of taking my customary seat, which was three stools away from the stranger, I saw right beside him. He took no notice of me, but continued to drink his coffee in silence.

"I thought perhaps you'd left town," I said to him. "I didn't see your truck around anywhere."

"I did leave town," he answered. "Now I'm back again."

"Did you find what you were looking for?" I made a guess.

He turned to me. he had the deepest, blackest eyes I'd ever seen. They seemed to reach beyond his soul into the graves of his ancestors. "No."

"I wish I could say I was sorry," I said.

He grunted and went back to drinking his coffee.

That angered me. Whenever I thought we were getting somewhere, he just clammed up. "You're the interloper here," I said, trying to draw him out. "In case you haven't noticed."

"The Indian always is . . ." He paused to casually survey the Corner Bar and Grill, stopping at each booth in turn until its occupants looked away. ". . . in the white man's world." Apparently satisfied that everyone was sufficiently cowed, he took another sip of coffee.

"That's a bunch of crap and you know it," I said. "Your being an Indian has nothing to do with it."

"What does then?"

"Being a stranger."

"Strangers aren't welcome in Oakalla?"

"Not for long. Not if they choose to stay that way."

"I choose to stay that way."

"Why? Because you want it that way?"

"No. Because that's the way it works out. If I tell you who I am, then you'll think you know why I'm here." He kept his eyes directed at mine so I wouldn't mistake his meaning. "And you'll be wrong."

Uninterrupted silence followed. Together we watched David Roberts enter the Corner Bar and Grill and march right past us into the bar without even a glance in our direction. "What do you think of that one?" I asked to break the ice.

"We have a saying in our tribe," he said. "No son can see his glory in the shadow of his father. I think that one would be happier somewhere else besides Oakalla."

"Your tribe being the Blackfoot?"

"No. I'm Cheyenne."

"Tom Two-Feathers was a Blackfoot."

"Was he? I wouldn't know."

"It's his truck you're driving."

"No," he corrected me. "It's my truck."

Late that night I finally had my column written and the *Oakalla Reporter* ready to print. Clarkie came into my office. I was surprised to see that he had little Jimmy Parker with him.

"What's going on?" I asked Clarkie.

"You'll have to ask him," Clarkie said. "I found him wandering uptown in front of the bank. He wouldn't let me take him home, so I brought him here."

"Is that true, Jimmy?" I said.

Jimmy didn't answer.

"Problems?" my printer asked, while thumbing through an old issue of *Sports Afield* that had somehow found its way from home to my office.

"Apparently so," I answered. "Go ahead and start without me, and if you have any questions, you'll find me here."

"Will do," he said on his way out.

Meanwhile Clarkie left too, leaving Jimmy and me

100

alone in my office. "You want to tell me about it?" I asked.

"No," he answered.

"Were you running away from home?" I noticed that his shoes were untied and that he was wearing pajamas under his jacket. He also carried his stuffed dog, Mickey.

"No."

"What were you doing then?"

"Trying to find my daddy." Tears crept into his eyes as he spoke.

"Why, Jimmy? Why were you trying to find your daddy?"

He didn't answer.

"Does it have anything to do with David?"

Jimmy frowned. "He's a bad man. He's trying to take my mommy away."

"Where is he trying to take her?"

He shrugged. "Somewhere. I've heard them talking."

"Does your daddy know about this?"

Looking down at Mickey, he tweaked his nose. "Yes."

"Because you told him?"

"Yes."

I put my arm around him. "Jimmy, think hard because this is important. Just what did you tell your daddy about this?"

He leaned against me and closed his eyes. "I'm tired. Can I go home now?"

"When you tell me what you told your daddy."

"Mommy won't like it."

"It doesn't matter whether your mommy likes it or not. I still need to hear it."

He looked up at me with those sad eyes of his and I could feel myself weaken. "Are you my friend?"

"Yes, Jimmy, I'm your friend."

101

"Friends aren't supposed to tell on each other."

"I won't tell on you, Jimmy. But I do need to know the truth."

"Why?"

"Because the truth matters. Without it we can't tell the good guys from the bad guys."

"My daddy is a good guy."

I tightened my hold on him. "I know he is, Jimmy." Grasping my arm in both hands, he lifted it from around him and slipped away from me. "You said you were going back to look for him."

"I am," I said. "Soon."

"When?"

"Day after tomorrow."

"You promise?"

"I promise."

As I waited for him to make up his mind whether to tell me or not, I closed my eyes and thought about all the things that I could have done and didn't do that week to make the *Oakalla Reporter* the cut-above-average newspaper I wanted it to be. And there I sat in my office with a five-year-old boy, waiting for an answer from him that might or might not be important, while the press of the *Oakalla Reporter* rolled without me. I wondered, if I ever got the chance to lecture a journalism class, what of value I had to tell them about setting priorities. Life had a way of setting its own.

"I told Daddy that Mommy planned to run away with David and he'd never see me again."

"What did your daddy say to that?"

"He said that nobody would ever take me away from him. He'd die first." Tears reappeared in Jimmy's eyes.

"Are you afraid that's what's happened to him? Is that why you went out looking for him tonight?"

He took a long time in answering. "Yes."

A couple of hours later I sat in my office chair with

my feet up on my desk, scanning that week's edition of the *Oakalla Reporter,* while my printer sat on my desk, reading my column. Jimmy was covered with my old army blanket and lay asleep on the cot I kept in my office for those times when I knew I wouldn't make it home to bed. But he hadn't been there long. First he had to see how everything worked, including my hot plate, stapler, and pencil sharpener. Then he and Mickey had to take turns spinning in my swivel chair. Neither he nor Mickey got that first bit dizzy, but I had to take time out from what I was doing to walk outside for a breath of fresh air.

Rowena Parker came into the office. As she did, my printer left to put the labels on the *Oakalla Reporter* in preparation for mailing.

"Have a seat," I said, offering her a chair.

"No, thank you. I think I'll just pick up Jimmy and go."

I'd called her the first chance I got to tell her where Jimmy was. She didn't believe me at first, not until she went into his bedroom and found his bed empty and his window open. Rowena had then taken two hours in getting here. "Have a seat," I repeated.

Her dark eyes flashed with anger. "Look, I've got to go to work in the morning. I've got appointments at . . ."

I cut her short. "I really don't give a damn what you have to do. Sit down," I said.

She sat down nervously on the edge of a chair, as if ready to bolt at the first opportunity. "David's out in the car," she said.

"I don't care. He can wait too."

"If it's about Jimmy," she said, "well, you just don't understand."

"I understand that I called you two hours ago to tell you Jimmy was here. Where in the hell have you been?"

"Don't you start on me!" she snapped. "You're not his mother. You're not his anything that I can see."

"You're right. I'm not," I said. "And I don't pretend to be. But since you are his mother, maybe you can tell me why he ran away tonight."

"He's confused," she answered. "All this business about his father has got him upset." She looked to where Jimmy was sleeping on the cot. "And bringing him here doesn't help any."

"I didn't bring him here. He was brought to me."

"That's what you say," she said.

"That's the truth, like it or not."

She rose from the chair. "It doesn't matter whether it's the truth or not. I'm Jimmy's mother and I'm taking him home."

"You know what you're about to do is kidnapping in this state."

She stopped. Then she took a couple of steps and turned to face me. "I don't know what you're talking about. I'm taking Jimmy home, that's all."

"You're planning to leave the state with him without his father's permission, and that's kidnapping."

"Who told you that?" She wore an ugly scowl, as if she'd been caught in a lie and she knew it. "Jimmy did, didn't he? Well, you can't believe anything the little liar says."

"Rowena, shut up," I said. "I'm tired. You're tired. We neither one like each other very much right now. So just take Jimmy and go. I still have work to do tonight."

"Don't order me out," she said, retreating to the chair she'd vacated earlier. "Without hearing my side of it."

"I thought I had heard your side of it. Jimmy's a little liar, and I'm a meddling bastard. Or have I left anything out?"

"I didn't mean that about Jimmy," she said. "Or you either. And anyway, I never called you a bastard. I just wanted you to listen to me without making any judgments."

"I wasn't making any judgments. I just couldn't understand why it took you two hours to get here."

"That doesn't make me a bad mother," she said. "I knew that Jimmy was in good hands and that he didn't want to see me, or you would have brought him home instead of leaving him here. What was I supposed to do when you called, rush right over here and apologize to him about his running away and scaring me to death? What would you have done, if you had been me?"

"I honestly don't know, Rowena. But I think I might have gotten here sooner than you did."

"Even if you had, what would that prove? You've cared for Jimmy for a few days now. I've cared for him all his life. There were months and months when I was the only one who did care for him. Not his father, who was always out digging in an Indian mound somewhere. Not David, who was too much in love with himself to care about me or anybody else." She stopped to take a deep breath. "Not you and the rest of this town, who could have cared less what happened to Jimmy and me."

"In what way didn't we care?" I asked. "Were you starving, without food and shelter?"

"No!" she shouted. "I was trapped. Trapped and lonely, with a sickly baby that cried himself to sleep every night." Her eyes bespoke her anger. "Or weren't you listening on those nights we talked up at the Corner Bar and Grill?"

"I was listening," I said. "But I don't ever remember your telling me that. Mostly you talked about your life since your divorce, about how much you hated being a beautician and what you wouldn't give to finally get out of Oakalla for good."

"Are you sure I didn't tell you about Jimmy and me? I thought I had."

"If you had, I honestly don't remember, Rowena.

105

And that's not because I've chosen to forget. Usually I remember things like that. I'd make a piss-poor friend if I didn't."

She looked as though she wanted to believe me. "Who ever said we're friends?" she asked.

"I did," I said. "At least I always thought we were."

"Then why did you stop coming to the Corner Bar and Grill?" she said. "And why didn't you ever ask me out on a real date?"

"I stopped coming to the Corner Bar and Grill," I told her, "because I was drinking too much and spending too much time up there feeling sorry for myself. As for the reason why I never asked you out on a real date . . . well, that's not as easy to answer."

"You can try," she said.

I could try, I thought to myself. But I doubted that she'd like what I had to say. "You know about Diana," I began.

"Yes, I know about Diana," she said sharply. "But according to what you told me, it was over between you."

"It was," I said. "And is," I felt compelled to add. "But it isn't. Not completely. Part of me still remembers how it once was between us and wants that back again. The other part of me knows that's impossible, and that it always will be. So in the meantime, until I sort it all out, I don't want to get involved with anyone else."

"We didn't have to get involved," she said, then laughed at her own boldness. "You know what I mean. We made it pretty clear there in the Corner Bar and Grill what our needs were."

"Mine still are," I said. "They haven't changed any."

"Then why didn't you ever try to make love to me?"

"It wasn't because I didn't want to."

"That's not an answer and you know it."

"Because," I said, hating the way it sounded. "To me making love is just that, making love. All of me needs to be involved, not just the otherwise essential parts. Be-

106

cause to me love is the most essential part." I smiled at her. "I'm sorry."

I thought that she would be hurt. Instead, she seemed relieved. "Thank God," she said. "I thought maybe it was my breath or something." She smiled back at me. "But you really did find me attractive?"

"Extremely."

"And it really was hard to say no to me?"

"Very hard."

"Tell me the truth now."

"I am telling you the truth, Rowena. For several weeks there last fall, that's all I could think about."

We exchanged a knowing look. "Yeah, me too." She sighed, letting her guard all the way down. "Until David came back."

I felt then a tightness in my chest; it was familiar by this time because it happened whenever the subject of David Roberts came up. "What exactly has David been telling you anyway? The last I heard he ran out on you several years ago."

She smiled the way Diana used to smile at me, as though we were the only two people on earth. It made me wish I hadn't said anything, because I knew that smile was meant for David Roberts. "David says he made a mistake by leaving me, but that's all behind us now. He also says he's willing to get a job to help put me through college, which is something I've always wanted to do. But he also wants me to sell the shop and move to California with him. And I don't know how willing I am to take that big a chance."

"On him or yourself?" I asked.

"On either one of us."

"And where does Jimmy fit in David's plans?" I asked. "Does he want to take Jimmy to California with you?"

"I'm not exactly sure where Jimmy fits in David's plans," she said. "David says he's willing to take Jimmy

107

too, if that's what I really want. But it would be a lot easier if it were just the two of us."

"What did you say about that?"

"I said," she answered, with resolve, "that I wouldn't give up Jimmy for anything. Not even him."

"And what was his answer?"

She stared at Jimmy. I thought I saw a hint of fear on her face. "'We'll see' was his answer." She rose from the chair and gathered Jimmy into her arms.

I held the door for her as she started outside where David Roberts sat in his white Corvette with the motor running. "David wouldn't hurt Jimmy, would he?" I asked.

She didn't answer.

"Rowena?"

She wouldn't look at me. "I'd better go. David has been awfully patient about this."

"The hell with David. I asked you a question."

As she turned my way, the lines seemed to soften around her mouth. "No. I honestly don't think so."

A couple of minutes later the Corvette sped away.

10

Friday came and went quietly. Friday evening I went to the Corner Bar and Grill for supper, where I once again encountered the stranger, who along with the rest of the regulars there had a bottle of beer in front of him and little or nothing to say. Then I went to see Rupert and Elvira.

Elvira opened the door and said that Rupert had already gone to bed.

"When was the last time he went to bed before nine on a Friday night?" I asked.

"When was the last time he went to bed before nine period?" she answered. "Would you like to come in and keep me company? I'm lonelier with him here than when he's out and about."

"Maybe some other time, Elvira."

She smiled sadly and said, "That's okay, Garth. I know who the real star of this household is."

"It's not that, Elvira. I can't go in there with him in bed. It's not Rupert somehow."

Her sadness deepened. "I know the feeling."

I left and went home to an empty house where I fixed myself a highball, got out a stack of old photographs, and kept myself company.

Early the next morning Ruth and I sat across the kitchen table from each other without speaking. Since she'd gotten in late from bowling the night before and since I said I wasn't very hungry, she had fixed oatmeal instead of her usual ham and eggs. But since I liked ham and eggs even if I wasn't very hungry and gagged on oatmeal no matter how hungry I was, I wondered why she'd fixed it. Probably to get even with me for her running out of gas in Jessie.

I scooted my bowl of oatmeal to one side so I wouldn't have to look at it. "What's the matter now?" she asked.

"Nothing's the matter," I lied. "I'm just not hungry."

The phone rang. Sure that it was Rupert, I got up, bumped the table in my hurry, and nearly upset everything on it. "I knew you'd call," I said.

"How's that, Garth?" Clarkie answered. "I didn't know myself until a couple of minutes ago."

"What is it you need, Clarkie?" I couldn't hide my disappointment.

"I just wondered what time you wanted to leave for the Barrens. I've got to take a water sample and send it in before we do."

"We'll leave as soon as you can get here." Then I glanced out the window and saw Tom Two-Feathers' 1955 Chevy pickup parked along the street in front of my house. "On second thought, Clarkie, I'll meet you at the rear entrance to the hardware at exactly eight-thirty. Don't be a minute early or a minute late."

"Sure, Garth." He sounded puzzled. "Anything you say."

"What was that all about?" Ruth asked when I returned to the table.

I nodded toward the street where the pickup was parked. "Diversionary tactics."

She wasn't impressed. "You seem to be going to an

110

awful lot of trouble lately just to keep an old Indian from following you."

"He's not just any old Indian," I said.

"What is he then?"

"I don't know. But he's a Cheyenne driving a dead Blackfoot's pickup in the heart of Chippewa territory. That makes him more than just an old Indian."

She began to leaf through Judge Glick's copy of *Folklore of Wisconsin*. It had hardly left her side since I'd given it to her. She even read it while she was cooking, which was something she rarely did. "I think you've read too much into this," she said. "Especially that story about old Matatomahawk, or whatever his name is."

"His name's Matatomah," I said sourly.

She put down the book to look at me. "You don't really believe that story, do you? I've lived around here all my life, and I've never heard of either him or the Oakalla before. Have you?"

"No," I admitted. "But tell me this, Ruth: Where did the name Oakalla come from?"

"From the covered bridge that used to sit across Stony Creek there south of town. It was the Oakalla Bridge, built before the town even."

"And it's how old?"

"A hundred and ten years, give or take a few."

"Look at the date when *Folklore of Wisconsin* was published. It's 1853, if I remember right."

She opened the book to make sure. "1854. But what does that prove?"

"It proves that the book came before the bridge. So it could mean that the bridge got its name from the book, or rather from the Oakalla in the book."

She laid the book aside. "You'd have a hard time making that stand up in court."

"No harder than you would proving otherwise."

Reaching for her coffee mug, she asked, "What's your point?"

111

"I'm not making a point. Just keeping my options open." I rose from the table and looked outside to make sure that the pickup was still there. "By the way, you have any luck deciphering the handwriting on that envelope I gave you?"

"Some," she said, not yet ready to commit herself. "I might have something for you by this evening."

I was relieved to see that the pickup hadn't left. "Fair enough."

At exactly eight A.M. I left the house and walked to the Corner Bar and Grill, then through the Corner Bar and Grill and down the wooden steps to its wine cellar, keg room, and basement; through the door that led to the basement under Sniffy Smith's barber shop, and finally through the opening that led into the basement of Fritz Gascho's hardware. Fritz had once shown me that same route in reverse when we'd gone into the basement of the hardware in search of some old clay tile for my broken sewer line at home. Fritz also said that even though the passageway had existed for as long as the buildings themselves, hardly anyone in Oakalla knew about it.

"Morning, Fritz," I said, appearing at the top of his basement step.

Fritz had just opened his door for business and was taking an inventory of his rakes and hoes. "Morning, Garth," he answered without even looking my way. "What can I do for you?"

I told him what I needed and he got them for me, including two packages of the most powerful flashlight batteries he had in stock. "Put it on your bill?" he asked.

"Yes, put it on my bill."

I walked to the back of the hardware and pretended to look at aluminum ladders. At exactly eight-thirty and right on time, Clarkie pulled up behind the hardware and beeped his horn for everyone within

112

earshot to hear. I ran out the back door of the hardware and got into his patrol car with him.

"Where to?" he asked.

"Go down the alley beside the cheese plant, take a left, and cross Jackson Highway onto Fair Haven Road. Once you get on Fair Haven Road, don't waste any time getting out of town."

Clarkie slammed his patrol car into reverse, throwing gravel all over Fritz's back step. "Anything you say, Garth."

When we crossed Jackson Highway, we were already doing thirty. At Fair Haven Church, the tombstones blurred by like confetti. Skyler's Woods evaporated into gray smoke and Willoby's Slough escaped me altogether. As we approached the junction of Fair Haven Road and Haggerty Lane, and Clarkie showed no sign in slowing down, I said, "There's a stop ahead."

"I know, Garth."

"Just ahead."

"I know, Garth."

"Then Goddamn it! Slow down!"

He slammed on the brakes, nearly throwing us into a tailspin. At that we slid through the intersection and half a car length into the field beyond. Instead of patiently working the car back and forth to get us out, he sat in reverse, spinning the tires.

I got out of the patrol car and walked around to his side. "We're stuck, Clarkie," I said.

He didn't agree. "I can get it, Garth. I almost have it now."

I watched the front end of the patrol car sink lower and lower into the wet field. Then I reached inside and turned off the ignition before he buried the car. "Give it up, Clarkie. It's a lost cause."

He reluctantly got out of the car and stood there in the middle of Haggerty Lane with a puzzled look on his

113

face. "I don't understand it," he said. "It's a front-wheel drive. They're supposed to go just about anywhere."

"Except through a plowed field in March."

A vehicle approached from the south. I hoped it wasn't a dark-blue 1955 Chevy pickup, or I would have been tempted to hide under the patrol car. Pete Hammond stopped in his green flatbed and asked, "Need any help?"

"What does it look like?" Clarkie answered.

I gave Clarkie a look that said to calm down. Knowing Pete, how wired he usually was and how easily upset, I didn't want Clarkie to set him off. Otherwise, we might have to wait until the next freeze to get out of there. "Yes, we could use some help," I said.

Pete flicked some ashes from his cigarette in Clarkie's direction. "I figured you might," he said, "after you went by my place like a bat. Where's the fire anyway?"

"No fire," I answered. "We were just trying out Clarkie's patrol car to see what it would do."

Pete shook his head and smiled, "When the cat's away . . ."

"Meaning what?" Clarkie took offense.

"You know what. With Sheriff Roberts laid up and all." Pete's smile faded. I could see trouble coming. Clarkie took his job seriously, even if no one took him seriously.

"Clarkie, we need you behind the wheel," I said. "Pete, if you have a chain handy, I'll hook us up and we can get out of here."

Pete Hammond made no move toward his truck. Clarkie made no move toward his patrol car. "Make that little twerp apologize first," Pete said.

"What for?" I said. "You insulted him."

"For impersonating a law officer." Then Pete smiled in jest.

Clarkie's jaw tightened and his ears turned a bright red, but to his credit he didn't say anything more to

Pete. Instead, he got into his patrol car, I hooked up the chain at both ends, and Pete pulled us out of the field.

"The sonofabitch," Clarkie said about fifteen minutes later when we were on our way again. "He'd never talk to me like that if Sheriff Roberts were around."

"No," I agreed, "he wouldn't. But Sheriff wasn't around."

"What's the difference, Garth?" he asked. "What's the real difference between Sheriff Roberts and me?"

"About thirty-five years' worth of experience for one thing," I said.

"Besides that."

I shook my head. I didn't know why some people naturally commanded respect while others didn't. "I honestly don't know, Clarkie," I said. I turned to look behind us and didn't see anyone following. "But I wouldn't worry about it."

"But I am worried about it," he answered. "I'm worried that Sheriff Roberts is going to die, or resign, and drop this job right into my lap. Then where will I be?"

"He's not going to die," I insisted.

"Resign then. And don't tell me that can't happen."

Clarkie had spoken my own fears. In answering him, I tried to answer myself. "It is a possibility that he might resign," I said. "Still, I don't think that will happen. One of these days he'll start to feel better. Then before long he'll be himself again. It's like having a bad cold that drags on and on. You don't think you'll ever get well. Then one day you are."

Clarkie wasn't convinced. "It seems to me it's a little more serious than that, Garth. Sheriff Roberts has a bad heart, not a bad cold."

"That's not what his doctor says," I replied. "It's not his heart, but the pressure he's under that's causing his chest pains."

"I know what his doctor says."

115

"Then why don't you believe him?"

"Because I'm scared," he admitted. "I couldn't be more scared than if he were my own father." Clarkie's face showed just how scared he was. "Not that I couldn't somehow manage without him. But I sure wouldn't want to try."

"I know, Clarkie," I said. "I feel the same way."

We entered the Barrens under a fair sky. What clouds there were drifted lazily from west to east without much wind behind them. The air was warm and the earth spongy underfoot as we walked from the cabin where Jimmy Parker's El Camino still sat up the valley toward the mouth of the cave.

"Here's where I leave you, Clarkie," I said when we reached the cave's mouth. "If I'm not out by sundown, go after help. Don't try to find me on your own."

"I still don't know why you won't let me go in there with you," he said. "In case you get into trouble."

"Because I'd rather have you out here," I said. "If one of us gets lost, chances are we both will."

He shrugged, showing his disappointment. "I guess you know best."

I stared at the mouth of the cave, which seemed to have narrowed since my first trip in there. "I'm not so sure about that."

I wore a hard hat with a miner's light mounted on it, the cord of the light inside my shirt and jacket, and its battery attached to a narrow belt around my waist. I also carried the biggest flashlight Fritz Gascho had in stock and three extra heavy-duty batteries in my pockets. Entering the cave, I went as far as I dared before I turned on the miner's light for the first time. As I watched its light shine on the walls of the cave, it didn't seem nearly so bright as it had in the hardware. It was bright enough, however, for me to see the dead deer lying on the floor of the cave a few feet ahead.

Someone had cut off the hindquarters of the deer

and left the rest of it there. Aiming my light into its bright dead eyes, I saw that it was a spike buck probably no more than a year old. Whoever had killed him had apparently cut his throat and then dragged him into the cave to butcher him. His entrails lay in a thick pool of blood that still seemed to seep from his body. I touched my finger to the blood. It was cold.

I went on. The cave continued to grow. I soon came to a crystalline chamber about ten feet wide and twenty feet long that looked like something out of Edgar Allen Poe. Unusually cool, with a rusty mural-like stain on one wall and what appeared to be a silica gargoyle imbedded in the other wall, it had a high arched ceiling, and two arched passageways leading from the far end of it. As I stood before the passageways trying to decide which one to take, I decided that I didn't much want to go either way.

I chose the one on the left and began to descend deeper into the earth, as the chill also deepened around and within me. Like crypts from the time of Creation, which entombed the earth as it formed, each succeeding chamber contained bonelike stalacitites and stalagmites, jeweled clusters of quartz and feldspar, and garish smears of orange and red clay, nature's first watercolors. Nowhere did I see man's mark on either the floor of the walls or the cave, and I felt, as surely as I once had on the shore of a pristine lake deep in Ontario, that I was among the first to enter there.

Then a strange thing began to happen. No matter how brightly my lights shone, and I had turned on both the flashlight and the miner's light, they couldn't penetrate the dense darkness ahead. Something in the walls of the cave, as they began to bend and constrict, swallowed light.

I took a few steps and stopped. There I thought I heard water for the first time. It wasn't the sound of a trickle from a spring quietly dripping through a crack in the rock, but rather the rush of a rapids that seemed to come from somewhere below me.

Kneeling and putting my ear to the floor of the cave, I could hear the sound much more clearly and determined that it was water I heard and not a gust of wind from somewhere outside the cave. Fascinated, I lay listening for several minutes before I went on.

Another sound came from behind me. It was sharp and close and sounded like rock scraping against rock. Then a too familiar smell seized me and stopped me in my tracks, the smell of rotten eggs.

Momentarily I left it behind, then encountered a sharp dense pocket of it that threatened to take my breath away. Holding my hand over my nose and mouth in order to breathe, I had taken only a few steps when something suddenly roared at me. I stopped and shined my flashlight on the floor of the cave; then I took a step back. Less than a yard away, the yawning mouth of a pit, which stretched nearly from wall to wall, belched the foul odor of hydrogen sulfide. And somewhere far beneath the pit, a mighty river flowed.

I couldn't go on, I decided. But when I turned to retreat, I saw a figure standing in the cave a few yards behind me. Surprised by the light, he slipped back into the darkness, which lay just beyond the reach of my flashlight. Whoever he was, I didn't trust him. He had come shadowy and silent from somewhere within the cave to follow me.

Trying not to look down, I tested the narrow rim of rock around the pit. It seemed solid enough to hold my weight, but I would have to traverse it in the dark because I couldn't see much with my face against the wall. Even at that my first step nearly proved disastrous. I'd turned my hard hat around and put my flashlight in my back pocket so that I could get closer to the wall of the cave, but I forgot about the battery on my belt, and as it bumped against the wall, it nudged me backwards.

Straining to regain my balance, I made the mistake of looking down and caught a blast from the pit squarely in the face. For a moment I couldn't breathe and lost all sense of where I was. When I regained my bearings again, I found myself with my head turned sideways and my nose flat against the wall, afraid to move. Sliding my battery around to my back didn't help any. Nothing helped, and I kept going only because I feared the pit less than I feared staying there within easy reach of whoever was behind me.

It took forever, it seemed, for me to inch my way across the pit. With each step possibly my last, I tried to make too sure of it until I reached the point where my feet and legs went numb, and I could hardly move. Then the ledge seemed to turn to ice, and I felt as if I skated the last yard on stilts before I reached the other side.

With an ear to the wall of the cave, I listened for whoever was following me. What I heard raised the hair on my nape. High and thin, more of a whine than a bark, his cry spoke of his fear and frustration on encountering the pit. But what set me on my way was the undertone of savagery beneath the cry.

Still unable to see more than a few feet ahead of me with both lights burning, I shut off the miner's light and used only the flashlight. Then I stepped from nearly total darkness into space, domed overhead, that reminded me of a cathedral; everything glistened. It was a large white honeycombed with many small crystal chambers that were stacked one upon the other like jewels in a vault. Pausing a moment to take it all in—something so rare and so grand that I very likely would never see anything like it again—I wished that I had all the time in the world to explore each chamber and see what wonders might be hidden there. But whether I imagined it or not, I thought I heard some-

119

one in the cave behind me. Circling the walls of the dome with my light, I felt a stab of panic when I saw no way out. Even if there were no one in the cave behind me, the thought of crossing the pit again left me weak.

Something scraped the wall of the cave. It sounded like the same sharp something that had scraped the wall of the cave earlier. I turned off my light, crawled into the nearest chamber, and waited there in the dark. Seconds later I heard someone enter the dome and stop just a few feet away from me.

Sniffing loudly as if trying to smell me out, he stopped at each chamber in turn and scraped something hard and sharp along each of its walls. As he circled the dome, I began to move with him, keeping a few chambers behind. That worked for exactly three times, until I realized he'd done an about face and was headed back my way, probing here and there at random.

With as many chambers as there were in there and the odds of his finding me in my favor, I knew from my previous hunting experience that the best thing to do was to sit tight and wait him out. The pheasant that flushed usually got shot. The pheasant that sat tight usually got a second chance at life.

But I remembered one time in particular on a snow-swept Indiana prairie when a cock pheasant, who was old enough to know better, made the mistake of trying to wait me out. What he didn't realize was that longtime rabbit hunter and mediocre shot that I was, I was used to kicking every brushpile, every brier, bush, and every clump of tall grass because I had to give myself every advantage or go home empty-handed. So there we came to be, the cock pheasant crouched under some millet with his long tail sticking out, and I standing over him with Grandfather Ryland's Model 97 Winchester at the ready. And I thought how stupid of him. He should have fled the territory when he had the chance.

120

But I never got the chance to run. Someone entered the chamber right beside me and began to furiously rake the walls with what I determined was a knife of some kind. He seemed to be growing increasingly frustrated and I thought that if I could sit for a few more minutes, he might give up and move on. So I made myself lie there and wait.

He came into the chamber where I lay and began to scrape the walls with his knife. Sparks flew from the wall as he circled the chamber. Then he stood over me, his bare feet inches away from my face. Afraid of what he might do next, I reached out and tripped him. Something hard clattered to the floor, as he fell back against the wall of the chamber and spun away from me. I felt along the floor of the chamber until my hand struck something sharp and knife-like. But it had apparently fallen from his belt and not from his hand because its handle was smooth and cold, like ice.

He'd left the chamber. Realization came in the form of a long deep silence that seemed to hold even the river beneath me at bay. Then he reentered the chamber where I was, darting in and darting out before I could even react, and returned the way he'd come. Another silence followed. When I thought he'd left the dome for good, I turned on my flashlight and began to search for a way out.

One of the lower chambers at the far end of the dome turned out to be a tunnel, and the tunnel soon began to climb toward what I hoped was daylight and Clarkie. I stepped on something hard that rolled out from underfoot, lost my balance, and took a hard fall. Then I had to slap my flashlight with the heel of my hand a couple of times to get it to work again.

Shining my light on the floor of the cave to see what had tripped me, I found another flashlight. It had a broken lens and what looked like dried blood smeared on it. On the floor of the cave itself was a large smear of blood, some of it still tacky, and bits of glass from the broken lens. I found another smaller smear of blood a short way up the cave, then another a few yards farther on. It seemed, from what I'd seen so far, that someone had fallen in the cave; then he had either walked or dragged himself out, leaving the smears of blood where he rested.

I came to a spring, which ran through a crack in the cave toward the river below. As I knelt to drink my fill, I noticed some dead minnows lying at the bottom of the small rock basin where the water pooled before it began its descent. The dead minnows bothered me. What bothered me even more was that the water had a bitter taste to it. I spat out what I had in my mouth and went on.

The cave then began to shrink, and I had to crawl on my hands and knees in order to get through it, as I had at the beginning. Since it was no longer any use to me, I put my flashlight in my belt alongside the other flashlight I'd found and went on in the dark. I wondered, as my climb abruptly steepened, why I didn't see daylight. By Garth's calculations, based solely on the seat of his pants, I should have been nearing the end of the cave. I found out why when my right hand struck a large rock. Someone had sealed the entrance.

At first, when I thought about how far I'd come and how it would be hard, if not impossible, to retrace my steps, I wanted to lie there and cry. But I could see Grandmother Ryland, wagging her finger in my face as she had so many times in the past, admonishing me to quit feeling sorry for myself. "Don't sit there and cry about it," she'd say. "If you don't like it, do something about it."

What? I wondered. If I had something to dig with, I might be able to dig myself out. But a flashlight made a poor shovel.

122

Then I realized that I did have something to dig with. I held it in my left hand and had carried it all the way from the dome. Already it fit my hand so well I didn't even know it was there.

11

I emerged from the cave and collapsed on the ground, exhausted, staring at the sky and watching the clouds drift by overhead. Shadows had overspread the hillside where I lay, and even without looking at my Timex, I knew that it was late afternoon or evening and that I should set out to find Clarkie before it got dark. Still I remained there for several minutes without moving. It felt good just to be outside and on earth again.

Whoever had put the rock there to seal the mouth of the cave had to be large and strong. He had lifted a rock weighing at least three hundred pounds from its resting place, carried it thirty yards uphill, and put it exactly where he wanted it. He also had been careful to cover his tracks. Though I searched the entire hillside, I found nothing to tell me where he'd come from or where he'd gone. Not back into the cave, I surmised. Not unless he crawled in and closed the cave behind him.

A couple of hundred yards from the mouth of the cave I discovered something that didn't entirely surprise me. Hidden in a deep ravine, and covered with freshly cut brush and tree limbs that someone had obviously

124

put there, were several rusty barrels of what we determined later was cyanide and sulfuric and nitric acid, along with some small thick plastic kegs of muratic acid. Most of the barrels were still intact, but a few had ruptured, possibly in the earthquake, and spilled their contents into the ravine.

A new blue barrel caught my eye. Rolled into the deepest part of the ravine and covered with a small cedar, it had escaped my notice until I moved the cedar while trying to uncover another barrel. I righted the new barrel with some difficulty and then hesitated to open it. Something solid had moved inside when I righted it. It turned out to be Judge Glick.

At least I guessed that it was Judge Glick. White and shrunken, his face looked too small for his dark green eyes which seemed in death to have grown larger with a new awareness. Horror showed in them, as though Judge Glick had encountered something beyond all logic and reason, and certainly beyond his power and control. I wondered what he'd had in mind by coming here in the first place. Was his plan to confront whoever had killed him? Whatever it was, he had overestimated his ability to accomplish it.

Climbing to the top of the hill above the ravine where the barrels lay, I looked for Clarkie and saw instead long rays of orange sunlight glinting off of the top of a blue building in the next valley south of me. I thought I also saw a gravel road leading into the building and the dust of someone leaving the building. I hoped that it wasn't Clarkie.

The blue metal building had a high woven wire fence around it, three strands of barbed wire on top of that, and a padlocked gate. After walking all the way around the fence without finding a way inside, I stopped at the gate. Printed in bold black letters was a sign that read: *KEEP OUT!* Below printed in smaller black letters, was: *This means you.* Below that, printed in

125

red paint, was the message: *If you think I'm kidding, come on in!!* I climbed the gate and went on in.

I looked everywhere, but I couldn't find a way into the building, which was solidly built and padlocked like the gate. I couldn't even find a peephole in the metal, or the slightest crack that would let me see what was inside.

After climbing back over the gate, I began to walk along the gravel road in search of Clarkie. In the valley, as the clouds went from orange to red to purple to lavender, and the sky faded to the color of old jeans, it appeared the sun had already set and dusk was only moments away. But the surrounding hills still wore an orange glaze, and as I climbed out of the valley, I soon discovered that the sun still sat just above the horizon—an orange, then red orb that slowly began to sink out of sight.

"It's a good thing I didn't listen to you," Clarkie said. "Or you might still be wandering around here in the dark."

Clarkie had found me by chance as I walked along the gravel road about three miles from where I'd started that morning. I doubted that I'd walked that far in the cave, at least as the crow flew, but I had walked far enough to lose my bearings and get lost. I told him to drive back to the building that I'd just left.

"When did you start looking for me?" I asked.

We had arrived at the metal building and Clarkie stopped in front of the gate. "It was around five o'clock," he said, glancing at his watch. "I figured that since you hadn't come out yet, you were either lost or had come out somewhere else. Either way I didn't see the harm if I came looking for you."

"I'm glad you did," I said. "It would have been a long walk home."

He eyed the padlocked gate, then the building itself. "If you don't mind me asking, what are we doing here?"

126

"We came to pick up a passenger."

He shined his spotlight on the building and the surrounding area. "Then where is he?"

"Around back a ways. I'll show you."

I'd forgotten about Clarkie's queasy stomach. He threw up several times before we could get Judge Glick to the car, and would've thrown up more if he'd had anything left in him. Likewise, I had to stop a couple of times to take short walks before I could continue.

"Remind me not to pack a lunch next time," he said when we finally laid Judge Glick in the trunk. "At least not with dill pickles and deviled eggs in it."

"I'd just as soon not talk about lunch right now."

"Where to from here?" he asked as we got into the car.

"Doc Airhart's."

"What about Sheriff Roberts? Shouldn't we tell him first?"

"We can tell him what we know as soon as we leave Doc's."

"Will somebody let me know?" He sounded hurt.

"Know what, Clarkie?"

"What went on in that cave today."

"What makes you think anything went on?" I ran my fingers along the blade of the knife I'd carried from the cave. I didn't want to put it down, even though I no longer needed its protection.

"The way you smell for one thing," Clarkie said. "You smell like the water back in Oakalla. For another there's a strange look in your eyes. It's kind of spooky," he said as his own eyes began to widen. "And then there's that knife you won't let go of, like it was magic or something."

"It's not a knife," I lied. "It's a piece of flint I found on the floor of the cave."

"It's a knife, Garth," he said, turning on the dome light. "Here, take a good look at it."

127

At Clarkie's insistence I held the knife out in front of me to examine it, even though I already knew it by heart. Truly a work of art, it was an intricately cut and highly polished piece of white quartz that sparkled at every facet like a giant crystal. I would have given almost anything to have known the man who made it. "You're right, Clarkie," I said. "It is a knife."

"And where did you really get it?"

"In the cave, like I told you. Someone dropped it and I picked it up."

"*Who* dropped it?" he persisted. "I thought you went in there alone."

"I did. He was already in there."

Then I told him all that had happened in the cave. When I finished, he just sat there, staring straight ahead at the road. "If you're trying to scare me, Garth, you're doing a good job of it," he said.

"I told you the truth, Clarkie. If I hadn't been there, I wouldn't have believed it myself."

His eyes began to water. "What do you suppose it was that followed you?"

"Not a what, Clarkie. A who. A man followed me. That much I'm sure of."

"You saw him then?" Clarkie wasn't convinced.

"I saw enough of him to know what I'm talking about."

Clarkie was silent for several minutes, then said, "But what kind of man, Garth, would live in a cave?"

I looked at him and shrugged. I had been asking myself that same question.

When we got to Oakalla we pulled all the way in to Doc Airhart's drive and stopped in front of his garage. Clarkie stayed in the car while I knocked on Doc Airhart's back door.

"Coming!" he yelled from somewhere inside. "You don't have to break the damn thing down."

Doc Airhart was the closest thing we had to an

128

institution in Oakalla. He had lived there for over fifty years, ever since he and his wife, Constance, had moved to Oakalla from Cleveland in the early 1930s. Constance had died the year I moved to Oakalla and Doc had given up his medical practice that same year in favor of fishing and gardening. But recently, because he said that he had nothing better to do, Doc had begun to write his memoirs. Though I'd tried to get him to let me print some excerpts in the *Oakalla Reporter*, Doc said that he wouldn't allow that until he was dead and buried. Then he didn't give two hoots what happened to them.

Doc opened his back door, took one look at who it was, and slammed the door in my face. "I'm not here," he said. "Come back tomorrow."

I waited for him to open the door again. "Thank you," I said, stepping inside.

Short, white-haired, and wiry, with a ready smile and merry blue eyes, Doc had seemingly boundless energy, and his ongoing love affair with life still saw the roses. He and I fished together whenever we could and took one day every October to go grouse hunting. Lately, though, it seemed we'd spent too much of our time together looking at old bones.

"I know it's trouble," he said. "Back door or front door, I know it's trouble whenever you show up."

"What if I said I'm just here to visit."

"You'd be a liar," he answered. "So get on with it. I'm about to finish 1939 tonight." His brows raised momentarily as he frowned at me. "Or was."

I held the back door open for him as we went outside. "I know that deep down in your heart you're really glad to see me."

"Like hell I am."

Clarkie handed me the keys and I opened the trunk for Doc to look inside. Then he just stood there shaking his head. He was at a momentary loss for words. "I swear, Garth," he said, finding his voice again. "I don't

129

know how you keep coming up with these, but I wish you'd take them somewhere else when you do."

"It's Judge Glick," I said.

"I know who it is," he snapped. "I've known the man most of my life. And there's not a better man around." He turned back to the trunk and shook his head sadly. "At least there didn't used to be. He got sort of addled in his old age."

"No danger of that happening to you," I said.

"No," he agreed. "No danger of that happening to me." Then he turned his gaze to Clarkie, who was trying to avoid it. "Don't sit there like a bump on a log, Chief Deputy Clark. Help us get the Judge inside."

While Doc went down to his basement where his office used to be, I sat in his living room on the floor, petting Belle, Doc's old English setter, who in dog years was even older than Doc. Clarkie had gotten a call on his radio about an accident south of town, and he'd gone to investigate it. Meanwhile I had called Ruth and told her where I was and where I was headed next. But I didn't tell her about Judge Glick. I thought I'd better save that until I got home.

Belle groaned and rolled over on her back so that I could scratch her belly. Soon her right hind leg kept time with my hand, going ever faster the faster I scratched. Doc came up from the basement and stood in the doorway watching us. His old eyes looked both sad and amused.

"I see you're busy spoiling her again," he said.

"She's come to expect it."

"From me too. That's the trouble."

I rose from the floor. Belle whined as I did, holding all four legs straight up until I petted her again.

"You see what I mean," he said.

I followed Doc into his kitchen where he put on a pot of coffee. "You hungry?" he asked.

I hadn't thought about it until then. "Yes."

He opened his refrigerator and began to rummage through it. "How does leftover corned beef and cabbage sound? I don't have much else," he said. "Belle eats what I don't."

"Corned beef and cabbage sounds wonderful." At that point I'd have eaten anything, even liver and onions if he'd offered.

He put the corned beef and cabbage in a pan, set the pan on the stove, and sat down across from me while he waited for the coffee to perk. "You outdid yourself this time," he said. "You must lay awake nights trying to figure out firsts for me."

"I'd think, in all the years you were coroner, that you'd have seen at least one person before who'd been stabbed to death."

"That I have," he said. "Several of them in fact." Then he picked up the quartz knife that I'd laid on the table in front of me. "Where did you get this?" he asked, turning it back and forth as the light played upon it.

"In the cave. Why?"

He laid the knife back down on the table, although, like me, he seemed to have a hard time letting go of it. "Nothing," he said. "I must be losing something in my old age, because for a minute there I thought I'd found whatever it was that killed Judge Glick."

I let the knife lie on the table. "I don't see how it could have been *this* knife," I said, feeling the need to defend it.

"Never said it was." He rose to pour the coffee. "But that's the closest I can come to it." He set a cup of coffee at his place and one in front of me. "There's two percent milk in the icebox and the sugar's already on the table," he said. He lifted a stack of mail and looked under it. "Somewhere."

I got the milk from the refrigerator and added a splash of it and a couple of teaspoons of sugar to the

131

coffee before tasting it. "The coffee's good," I said, pleasantly surprised.

"It ought to be," he said. "I had to drive fifty miles round trip for the water to make it. Then you come in here smelling like a sewer." He waved his hand back and forth a couple times to clear the air.

"Sorry," I said. "I got that in the cave where I found the knife."

He blew on his coffee to cook it. "Where is this cave you keep talking about?"

"It's over in the Barrens. Near where I found Judge Glick."

After taking a moment to think that over, he rose from the table and brought me the corned beef and cabbage. Then he picked up the knife again to examine it. "What are you looking for?" I asked.

"It can wait until you finish your supper."

When I had finished my supper, I said, "My compliments to the chef. I can't remember when anything tasted so good."

But Doc was preoccupied with the knife. He kept turning it over and over in his hand to see what patterns he could throw on the wall with it.

"Doc," I said, unable to stand it any longer. "What is it about the knife that fascinates you so?"

"You done eating?"

"I'm done eating."

He laid the knife down, but his hand still hovered over it, until with a noticeable effort he drew his hand away. "Judge Glick wasn't just stabbed to death," he said. "Somebody tried to scalp him."

I stared at him a moment, then looked down at the knife. "With this knife?" I asked.

"Or one just like it. I found some tiny flakes of silica in some of the Judge's wounds. And the wounds themselves weren't made by an ordinary knife, or at least not one with a steel blade. But I couldn't figure out what else would have made them until I saw your knife."

I didn't say anything. My thoughts were on the events in the crystal chamber where I found the knife. I could still hear the sound that it made as it scraped the wall above my head. Or the sound that its twin made. I couldn't think ill of my knife, no matter what Doc said.

"Something bothering you, Garth?" Doc asked.

"You say someone tried to scalp Judge Glick?"

"He nearly got the job done," he said, taking a drink of his coffee. "If he'd known what he was doing, he would have." He continued to stare at me. "Why does that bother you so? Beside the fact that we don't hear much about that sort of thing anymore."

I rose from the table, taking the knife with me. "Because I have reason to believe that Judge Glick was still alive when it happened." I didn't believe anyone had carried Judge Glick out of the cave, or I wouldn't have found such a pronounced trail of his blood inside the cave. I believed he had walked or crawled out of the cave on his own.

"You might be right, Garth," Doc said. "The Judge bled to death. None of those wounds were deep enough to kill him."

"That's a comfort," I replied. "I'm glad you told me."

Doc sat back in his chair with his cup of coffee in his hand. "One good turn deserves another."

12

I didn't go to Rupert's as I had planned; instead, I stuck my flashlight inside my jeans and went into the Corner Bar and Grill. Glancing first at the bar, then at the lunch counter, I noticed that there weren't many people in there for a Saturday night. I guessed that the stranger with the large thick ears and the large hooked nose, the one dressed all in black who sat hunched at the lunch counter staring at me, was the reason no one was there. I watched him as I dialed Rupert's home.

"I'm back," I said to Rupert after Elvira got him out of bed for me.

"Back from where?" Though he'd been in bed, he didn't sound sleepy to me.

"The Barrens."

A pause, then he said, "You went into the Barrens alone again?"

"No. Clarkie went with me."

"Where in the Barrens?" he asked.

"The cave that I told you about before."

That bothered him. Several seconds passed before he replied, "Garth, you took a foolish risk, you know that, don't you?"

The last thing I wanted at that point was to be lectured by him. "Damn it, what else was I supposed to do? Last night when I came to ask for your help, you were already in bed, where you were tonight."

"I might've been in bed, but I wasn't asleep."

"How in the hell was I supposed to know that?" I then noticed that the stranger seemed to have more than a passing interest in our conversation. "Look, I'm not alone here, and I don't feel much like talking anyway, so I'll fill you in later."

"When later?"

"Whenever you get tired of feeling sorry for yourself and decide to be sheriff again." I hung up and took a seat at the bar.

"What'll it be?" Hiram, the bartender, asked.

"A draft of Leinenkugels."

"Coming right up."

I felt someone's presence and looked in the mirror to see the stranger standing directly behind me. Something in his eyes said that he wasn't pleased with me.

"Where did you get that?" he asked.

"Get what?" I replied.

"That knife in your belt."

"None of your business."

He put his hand on my shoulder. It was a large, powerful hand. "I asked you a question."

I pulled away from his hand. "And I gave you an answer."

"This man bothering you, Garth?" Hiram had returned with my draft of Leinenkugels. The look on Hiram's face said that the stranger had worn out his welcome long ago.

"No, Hiram," I said. "We're just having a friendly discussion. In fact, Mr. Two-Feathers here was just about to buy me that beer."

"That'll be six-bits then," Hiram said to the stranger.

135

To everyone's surprise, he dug into his pocket and pulled out a dollar bill that he gave to Hiram. "Keep the change," he growled.

"Much obliged," Hiram said grudgingly before moving to the other end of the bar.

The stranger sat down beside me, occupying all the space between us. "That was a nice stunt you pulled, Ryland," he said. "What if I hadn't gone for it?"

I took a drink of my Leinenkugels. On a scale of one to ten, the Leinenkugels was a ten plus. "The important thing is that you did go for it." Taking the knife from my belt, I laid it on the bar in front of him. "How old do you think it is anyway?"

He examined the knife. A subtle change seemed to come over him as he did. He saw it through eyes that were generations older and wiser than mine. "There's no way of telling," he said. "I saw something like it once before in Arizona. That knife was over five hundred years old."

"What were you doing in Arizona?" I asked.

"The same thing I'm doing here. Traveling." Turning the knife over in his hand, he asked, for the second time, "Where did you find it?"

"In a cave."

"Where's the cave?"

"In the Barrens."

He put his hand down flat on the bar. It covered the knife. "Don't play games with me, Ryland. I'm not in the mood."

"I'm not playing games with you. I told you the truth, which is a hell of a lot more than you knew before I found the knife. If you want to find out where I got it, you can go out looking for the cave the same as I did. Instead of expecting me to lead you to it."

"You're a stubborn bastard," he said.

I took another drink of my Leinenkugels. "I've been told that."

136

He held the knife up to the light and watched fascinated as it threw tiny rainbows all around the barroom. "The Barrens, you say? I'm not familiar with that area."

"It's in eastern Adams County and includes a part of Red Lake County. It's about five miles square," I added.

"That's twenty-five square miles."

"More or less."

Palming the knife, he held it out in front of him to study it more closely. "It's a work of art," he said, his black eyes shining. "Can you imagine the skill and patience it took to make it?"

As Hiram came to refill my glass, I waved him away. "No, I can't." Taking the knife from him, I held it out in front of me. I loved to look at it, but even more I loved the feel of it. "I wish I could meet its maker."

He coveted the knife—I could see it in his eyes as I put it back in my belt. And had we not been in a public place, I imagined I would have had to fight him to keep it. "What do you plan to do with that?" he asked.

"I don't know yet."

"You have no right to keep it."

"I have as much right to keep it as you do to want it."

"You're a smug s.o.b.," he said, rising from the bar stool.

I shrugged. "Nobody's perfect."

The stranger picked up his ten-gallon hat and left the Corner Bar and Grill. I breathed a sigh of relief.

After waiting for Hiram to go into the kitchen after an order, I made my way down the wooden stairs and retraced the journey I'd made earlier that day. Once I reached the basement of the hardware store, I unzipped my fly and pulled my flashlight out of my jeans.

I then had to get out of the hardware store without being seen. The quickest way was to go out the front

137

door. But I didn't want to take the chance of meeting someone there along Jackson Street and having to explain myself. So I went out the back door and hoped for the best.

Once home, I went directly to the garage and got into Jessie, because I didn't want Ruth to know where I was going. Though the gas gauge said that I had a quarter of a tank—enough gas to get me to the Barrens and back—this didn't necessarily mean that I actually had a quarter of a tank. It meant that I might have as much as half a tank or as little as an eighth of a tank. Like everything else about Jessie, the gas gauge worked when it wanted to.

After a stop at Grandmother Ryland's farm to get what I needed, I parked Jessie just outside the padlocked gate to the metal building and made my way to the mouth of the cave two valleys over. There I filled in the hole I'd dug earlier, tamping the dirt down with my shovel until it was nearly as solid as it had been before.

Then I drove to the top of the hill overlooking the shack where I'd found Jimmy Parker. No one challenged me as I made my way up the valley toward the cave, and I heard no sounds from without or within the cave to tell me that I was anything but alone there. Yet I knew that I wasn't alone. Somewhere around—I wished I knew where—someone carried a knife just like mine, perhaps with Judge Glick's blood still on it.

I'd never used dynamite before. I wasn't even sure that I knew how to set and pack the charge. The closest I'd ever come to using dynamite were the cherry bombs and silver salutes that I'd used as a kid to blow up cans. But I use to watch Grandmother Ryland use dynamite to clear boulders from her fields. She said the secret was in the mud and in the placement of the charge rather than the size of the charge itself. To prove her point she used a single stick to shatter a boulder the size of a garden tractor. Taking her advice to heart, I'd taken

138

only one stick of dynamite, one fuse, and one blasting cap from the shelf in the pantry where she'd always stored them.

But when it came right down to it, I couldn't touch the match to the fuse. I had the stick of dynamite in place, packed into a small crevice at the mouth of the cave. I had the blasting cap set and the fuse run, and I was reasonably sure that I could blow the cave if I wanted to and seal it until the next earthquake came. But almost at the point of no return, when the match was already lit and an inch from the fuse, I blew it out.

I wondered whether I had the right to deny to someone else all of the beauty and majesty that I'd seen inside the cave. It seemed unconscionably selfish of me, and maybe presumptuous, to do this. Neither did I want to take the chance, however remote, of rupturing the barrels at the other end of the cave and having their contents spill into the river below. As I put my ear to the floor of the cave, only to hear the whistle of the wind, more thoughts came to me. No matter how much I wanted to seal the cave and keep myself from ever having to go in there again, I couldn't do it blindly without arriving at the truth of the matter first. I didn't know whether the person who had followed me had killed Judge Glick. Furthermore, I didn't know why he had followed me or what he was doing in the cave. Or for that matter, what Judge Glick himself was doing in there. I had the gnawing feeling that whatever I chose to do in this case would prove to be wrong, yet too many questions were still unanswered for me to take it upon myself to blow the cave. I unpacked and defused the dynamite, put it into a grocery sack, and headed home.

13

"Rupert called" was the first thing Ruth said to me when I got home. "He said he didn't care how late it was when you got in, he wanted you to call him back."

I looked at my Timex. It was way past midnight. Some people were probably still up hiding Easter eggs.

I sat down in my favorite chair, leaned back, and closed my eyes. The trip home from the Barrens had not been relaxing.

For one thing, I carried a live blasting cap wrapped in a rag in my pocket and a stick of dynamite sitting in a grocery sack on Jessie's backseat. For another, Jessie's gas gauge had showed empty all the way home. Then at the Oakalla city limits sign she began to sputter and belch, and she finally died in the alley about thirty yards from the garage. So I used the last of the lawnmower gas to run her on into the garage, where I took the stick of dynamite out of the sack and hid it inside a length of iron pipe lying on the floor. I carried the blasting cap inside with the intention of hiding it in one of my drawers upstairs. Come Fourth of July, I'd find something to do with it.

"Didn't you hear me?" Ruth asked. "I said Rupert

called." Wearing her housecoat and moccasins, Ruth sat in her chair with her usual stack of magazines beside her.

"I heard you," I answered. "I'm not in the mood to talk to him right now."

She picked up a magazine, glanced at the cover, and put it down again. "Well, you'd better get in the mood because he sounds like he means business."

"That's too much to hope for," I said, forcing myself to get up. "But I might as well see what he wants."

"Yes, Garth?" Rupert answered on the first ring. He sounded more in touch than he had for days. I was encouraged.

"Ruth said you called and wanted me to call back."

"We didn't get very far earlier this evening," he reminded me. "You never told me what you found in the Barrens."

"Judge Glick, for one thing," I said. "He's at Doc Airhart's in cold storage now." I looked at Ruth, who I saw was listening. I wished then that I had told her about Judge Glick before I made the phone call.

"Why at Doc Airhart's?"

"What you mean is why isn't he at the county coroner's, which is where you would have taken him. He's at Doc Airhart's because I needed some answers in a hurry and Doc's the best there is at giving them to me."

He took his time in answering, then said, "Why did you need them in a hurry?"

"A Garth emergency," I replied. "Or at least I thought there was. I was about to take the law into my own hands tonight when I decided otherwise. Maybe," I said, "because I couldn't be both the law and be above at the same time."

"I know the feeling," he said.

"I'm sure you do. So when are you going to relieve me of my duties?"

While I waited for him to answer, I watched a moth

141

buzz outside the kitchen window, wanting in. Meanwhile, Ruth padded into the kitchen and put on a pot of coffee. I didn't care what the water smelled like. Coffee seemed like a good idea to me.

"Any day now," Rupert answered. "I'm starting to feel like my old self."

"You're starting to sound like your old self too," I added, hoping to encourage him.

"It's not as much fun, is it, being the one in charge?" he asked.

"Not for me it isn't," I said. "But I think it is for you."

Once she had the coffee on, Ruth sat down heavily at the kitchen table and stared out the window. She looked sad and wistful, as if perhaps a sweet part of her past had just died.

Ignoring my last remark, Rupert said, "Judge Glick was one of the things you found in the Barrens. What was the other?"

"A dump of some kind. I think it contains some leaky barrels of cyanide among other things."

"In the Barrens?" He sounded puzzled.

"What better place for a dump?"

"But how did the cyanide find its way here?"

"By an underground river, I think."

"Have you seen the river?" he asked.

"Not exactly. But there in the cave I heard and smelled it. It smells exactly like our water does here."

"Did it always, I wonder?"

"I don't think so," I replied. "Not if it's the source of our water supply. It would have had to have happened since the earthquake."

"Then will it take another earthquake to get it right again?" We'd struck a sour note. He suddenly sounded tired and discouraged.

"It might take an earthquake to get the water tasting right again," I said. "But not to clean up the

142

dump and clear out the cyanide. We can start on that soon."

"Soon?" he said. "Why not tomorrow?"

"Because I want to get whoever's doing the dumping. If we go in there tomorrow and start cleaning it up, chances are we'll scare him off and never get another shot at him."

"But if we don't go in there tomorrow," he argued, "we run the risk of losing our water supply, and even the possibility of losing some lives in the bargain."

"I know that," I said. "But I still want to get him."

"It's not your decision, Garth," he reminded me.

"Then overrule me," I said in anger. "You're the sheriff."

"Just hold your horses a minute," he said. "I want to get whoever's been poisoning our water too. Maybe even more than you do. But I can't risk lives in order to do that, not the same lives I've sworn to protect. Do you understand that?"

I looked at Ruth. She was staring daggers at me. I didn't have to ask whose side she was on. "I understand what you're saying," I said. "And if I really thought somebody in Oakalla was going to die from drinking the water, I'd say okay, let's clean up the dump and to hell with whoever's behind it. But I don't think anybody's going to die because I've heard the river and I know there's an awful lot of water down there, too much for a few leaking barrels of cyanide to poison from an entry point fifteen miles or so away." I paused, collecting my thoughts. "And I also know that if we don't stop whoever's doing the dumping now, he'll start up again sometime in the future, somewhere else. And we'll have the same problem, maybe even a worse one, all over again. I don't want that to happen if I can help it."

"Maybe he won't start up again if we scare him bad enough," Rupert said.

"The person I have in mind doesn't scare easily."

"Who might that be?" he asked.

"The same person you've had in mind for some time now."

"Stub Timmons?"

"Yes. Stub Timmons."

"Do you think he's the one who killed Judge Glick?"

"I think it's a possibility. So you have to decide just what you want to do about it."

While he made his decision, Ruth got up and poured us each a cup of coffee, then took the half-and-half out of the refrigerator and set it and the sugar bowl on the table.

"There might be a simpler way to get to Stub Timmons," Rupert said. "If he owns that land where the dump is, then that's all we need to know to make a case against him."

"And if he doesn't own the land?"

"We'll cross that bridge when we get to it."

"Fair enough," I agreed.

"Any word on Jimmy Parker?" he asked, as I was about to hang up.

"No. I went into the cave looking for him, but I didn't find him, or any trace of him."

"What did you find in the cave, besides the river?"

I looked at Ruth who seemed to want an answer to that question herself. "Too much to go in to now."

"Are you planning to go back into the cave again?"

"Not unless I absolutely have to?"

"Why would you absolutely have to?" he persisted.

"To find Jimmy Parker."

"I thought he wasn't in the cave."

"He wasn't. At least not where I was," I said. "But it's a big cave, much bigger than I ever imagined."

"And if Jimmy Parker's not in the cave, do you have any idea where he might be?"

Two possibilities immediately came to mind. One was that he'd fallen into the same pit that nearly got me.

The other was that he was in one of the other barrels where I'd found Judge Glick. "Yes," I answered. "I have some idea of where he might be. But I don't want to speculate on that right now."

"When you do, let me know."

"You'll be the first." I hung up more encouraged than when I'd called.

"You stink," Ruth said as I sat down at the table.

"Thanks for the vote of confidence."

"I mean your clothes stink, like you've been rolling in something."

"It's from the cave," I said, adding sugar then half-and-half to my coffee. I tasted it and smiled. All things considered, the first sip wasn't too bad.

"Why didn't you tell me that you'd found Thorton?" Ruth asked. "I should have been the first to know." She didn't try to hide the fact that she was upset with me.

"I planned to tell you as soon as I got home, but I never got the chance."

"I don't mean just now when you walked in the door. I mean the first time you were back in town, before you stopped by home and tried to sneak that car of yours out of the garage without my hearing you." She sounded more hurt than angry.

After thinking of all the things that I could tell her, I decided to tell her the truth. After eight years together, I owed her at least that much. "Because I planned to blow up that cave I was in today. And I didn't want you or anybody else knowing about it."

"Why did you plan to blow up the cave?"

I told her why.

She nodded in understanding. She probably knew me better than anyone else.

"What about that cock-and-bull story you gave Rupert about Stub Timmons killing Thorton? You don't believe that any more than I do," she insisted.

"He's capable of it," I argued.

145

"That's not the point. You and I both know he didn't."

"Why didn't he?" I asked. "I'm almost certain that Stub put Judge Glick in that barrel where I found him. And I'm equally certain that Stub then drove Judge Glick's car back here to Oakalla where he searched Judge Glick's house and steam-rollered me in the process."

"You said there were two people in the house that night," Ruth replied.

"Yes, and my guess is that Isabelle Glick was the other one."

"And what were they searching for?" she challenged me.

"It wasn't *Folklore of Wisconsin*, as I first thought," I said. "It was that envelope with Judge Glick's handwriting on it that I asked you to decipher for me."

The look on Ruth's face said that my guess had hit home. She immediately got up from the table and began to water the plants in the kitchen.

"I'm right. Aren't I, Ruth?" I said.

"What if you are? Thorton's dead. What good will it do to start looking into his past for the reasons?"

I stared at her long enough to make her uncomfortable.

"And quit looking at me that way."

"Why are you soft-pedaling this, Ruth?" I asked. "Thorton Glick wasn't a god. In his later years he probably wasn't even a very good judge."

That brought a response. "Says who?"

"Says a lot of people, Rupert included. About nine or ten years ago he began to let things slide. Some people here in Oakalla say he even gave up caring whether he went to court or not. And when he did step down from the bench five years ago, it was no real surprise. It was a relief, more than anything else."

By then Ruth had heard enough. "Thorton Glick

was the best circuit court judge this county ever had," she said. "And I'll spit in the eye of anybody, including you and Rupert Roberts, who says otherwise."

"I'm only repeating what I've heard."

"Well, don't repeat it in front of me."

"Why? What was he to you?" I asked. "If not your lover, what?"

"I don't see how that's any of your business."

"Did Karl know about it?"

She spun around to face me. For a moment I thought she was going to throw her yellow plastic pitcher at me. "No," he didn't know about it," she answered. "Are you satisfied?"

I held up my hands in surrender. If she wanted to tell me anything more, she would; if she didn't want to tell me, she wouldn't. I'd said all I was going to. "Good night, Ruth. I'm going to bed," I said.

"No, you're not," she answered, dropping her pitcher in the sink and taking her seat at the table. "You're going to sit here and hear me out. It's the least you can do."

"Okay," I agreed. "It's the least I can do."

She took a sip of her coffee. It seemed to give her confidence. "Years ago," she began. "It's nearly fifty now. Thorton used to teach Sunday school at the Methodist church. Wait a minute," she said, rising from the table. "I think I have a picture of him then." She went upstairs and soon returned with a large black-and-white photograph. "I always kept this face down in the bottom of my hope chest because I was the only one who had the key."

I studied the photograph. The man in it was tall and straight, with wavy blond hair and a dreamy look in his eyes. He wore slacks, a white shirt open at the collar, and a deep all-weather tan that said he spent a lot of his time out of doors. Beside him, and equally as handsome, stood a tall, willowy woman, who wore blousey slacks, also a white shirt, also open at the collar, riding boots, and a look of contempt. Though the man looked strong and was in some ways the personification of manliness, I guessed that of the two of them, the woman was probably the stronger. Something in her eyes said so. Something in his eyes agreed with me.

"Who's the woman beside him?" I asked. "It's not you, is it?"

"Isabelle Glick."

She handed the photograph back to me. This wasn't the same Thorton Glick that I remembered from his later years. This one had more warmth and sensitivity. I thought I saw the reason why. In his early years, he didn't look like a judge to me, but more like a priest or a poet.

"You say you met him in Sunday school?" I asked.

"Yes. He taught the under-thirty class of young married and single people. I was a member. So was Karl, but he didn't go all that often. He always seemed to have something he needed to do on the farm."

"That sounds familiar," I said.

"Too familiar," she replied in reference to me. "Anyway, Thorton was a good teacher, but he had a hard time staying on the lesson, so we usually ended up talking about anything and everything. But I noticed that whenever he got serious and began to talk about matters of the heart and home, Thorton was usually looking at me. Then the next thing I knew he started slipping me poems that he'd written and wanted my opinion on." She smiled at something, perhaps at how easy it was. "Every week after class he'd hand his Bible to me and ask me what I thought about a particular scripture. The scripture was always marked by one of his poems."

"Were the poems any good?" I asked.

"I thought so at the time. But when they began to pile up, I told him flat out that I might have more of an

148

opinion on them if I knew who he had in mind when he wrote them. Otherwise, I had better things to do than wait for him every week after class so that he could show me a line of scripture."

"What happened then?" I asked when she didn't continue.

"Not much," she said. "That was about all there was to it. Karl somehow got wind of what was going on and started going to class with me every Sunday. Not long after that Thorton stopped teaching the class and pretty much dropped out of Sunday school altogether."

"Did Karl ever say anything to you about it?"

She shook her head. "Not that first word. But he didn't go to Sunday school a day longer than he had to either. As soon as Thorton dropped out, so did Karl."

I had to smile not only at Karl's perception, but also at his class in handling the whole matter. From what Ruth had told me about him, he sometimes knew her better than she knew herself.

"Did you ever try to see Thorton after that, or did he ever try to see you?" I asked.

"Not for a long, long time. Like I said, that was pretty much the end of it."

"Why not?"

"Why not what?" She'd picked up the photograph of Thorton and Isabelle Glick, but wasn't looking at it.

"Why didn't you try to see him again?"

"What was the point? I was married and determined to stay that way. Thorton and I both knew that."

"No other reason?" I thought that I hadn't quite heard the whole truth of the matter.

She laid the photograph in front of me. "Take a good look and tell me what you see."

"Thorton and Isabelle Glick."

"That's what I saw. What kind of a man would give his lady love, which I took myself to be, a picture of him with his sister in it?"

149

"Maybe a cautious one, in case it fell into the wrong hands."

"I'm inclined to think otherwise, considering what all he said in those poems he gave me."

"Then maybe it was the only recent photograph he had," I suggested.

"And maybe he had a whole drawer full of them with Isabelle in each and every one." She took a drink of cold coffee and set her cup down. "Not that there's anything wrong with being close to your sister any more than there is in being close to your mother. It's natural, I suppose, for most men to be one or the other. But I still want to see room for me between my man and the other woman in his life, whoever she may be."

"And you couldn't see that with Thorton?"

"No, I couldn't see that with Thorton. Something told me that even if I wanted him, which I wasn't sure I did, I'd have to battle Isabelle all of my life for him. I didn't think it was worth it."

"But you did see him again years later?"

"Yes. It was right after Karl died. I'd say no more than a month had gone by when Thorton showed up at my door with a dozen long-stemmed red roses in his hand wanting to take up where we'd left off." She looked disturbed. She hadn't quite gotten over it yet. "Nothing had changed for him, Garth. Not in forty years. He said he loved me, that he'd always loved me, and that he always would love me." She shook her head in disbelief. "And while I believed every word he said, I couldn't understand why nothing else in the world seemed to matter to him—not forty years of being a judge, or my marriage to Karl and the feelings I still had for him, or the fact that the most we had ever shared between us was a few of his poems when we were still in our twenties. That bothered me, Garth. In his mind we had never lived those years at all."

"Did you let him down easy?"

"I let him down. I can't say how easy it was."

"It was nine years ago, right, that Karl died?"

She frowned at me. She knew what I was getting at. "Nine years ago this July."

"Which was right about the time that Thorton gave up being a judge, for all practical purposes."

"I know that," she said sharply. "What's your point?"

"My point is, what then happened five years ago, when he quit being a judge altogether?"

Looking me straight in the eye, she said, "Do you really need to know?"

"Yes, Ruth, I really need to know."

"Hold on." She left the kitchen and returned with the envelope that I'd found in *Folklore of Wisconsin*. "I'll leave it up to you to figure it out," she said. "But every company that Thorton made a note of has one thing in common. Isabelle Glick kept their books for them at one time or another."

"Could she have been embezzling from them and Judge Glick found out about it somehow?"

"That could have been the case, but I doubt it."

I studied the envelope, noting the names, times, and dates. "I agree, Ruth. It had to be something else. Particularly if he kicked her out of his house because of it."

She yawned, then rose and dumped the rest of the pot of coffee down the drain. "Well, good luck figuring it out. I'm going to bed."

"Night, Ruth. I'll be heading that way myself shortly."

She stopped at the kitchen door. "You going to church with me in the morning?"

"Why? What's the occasion?"

"It's Easter."

"That's right. I almost forgot." I laid the envelope aside. It could wait until another day. "Sure, I'll go." I never went to church more than once or twice a year. It had nothing to do with anyone else or anything else except me and the way I was. Like almost every other public place, with the exception of restaurants and theaters, I enjoyed churches best when they were empty, and felt more at peace with God and me when we were alone.

I sat at the table for a few minutes longer, trying to find the energy to get up and go to bed. When I finally did get up, I did something I hadn't done in eight years, ever since I'd moved to Oakalla from Milwaukee. I locked both doors.

14

The next morning, Easter Sunday, Ruth and I sat in the next to the last row of the United Methodist church, trying not to look too conspicuous with our presence. In the row in front of us sat Elvira and Rupert Roberts, sharing the same hymnal, while Ruth and I each had our own. Ruth didn't sing at all and wouldn't pretend otherwise by opening her hymnal and mouthing the words. Rupert only sang the songs he knew and not even all of those, since he had two notes, high and low, that he could reach with regularity. I had three notes, high, low, and somewhere in between, so I pretty much followed Rupert's lead. Elvira, however, made up for all of us by singing everything loudly and well, including the amens along with the choir.

Directly to my left David Roberts and Rowena Parker sat with Jimmy Parker between them. Not one of the three looked happy to be there. Jimmy kept scooting against his mother and David kept dragging him off her. Rowena tried to stay aloof by ignoring both of them. Meanwhile, she kept twisting the large opal ring on her right hand as if it possessed some magical power that would make all of them disappear from view.

Isabelle Glick sat alone in the front row in a beige

suede suit and mink stole. It was strange to see her there without Judge Glick to balance her, like a single book-end on an empty shelf. He used to sit on the right aisle seat of the middle front row, while she sat on the left aisle seat of the same row. When the service ended, he went out the right side door and she went out the left, to walk, no matter what the weather, the eight blocks or so to their separate homes on opposite sides of Fair Haven Road. Without him there to balance her, her head seemed to tilt slightly to the right, as if she were listing in his absence—or perhaps listening for his fine tenor voice to keep her on pitch.

I didn't retain much of the sermon or the service that Easter Sunday. I enjoyed seeing the Easter lilies and the Easter suits again, but missed the Easter bonnets that the women and girls used to wear when I was a kid.

After the benediction and the choral amen, I left Ruth outside talking to Rupert and Elvira, waved to Doc Airhart who was raking his side yard, and started after Isabelle Glick. She reached the Marathon a few strides ahead of me, but I caught up to her in the next block, then walked another block beside her without speaking. She had a long, purposeful stride that outreached my own, even when I was in a hurry, and a no-nonsense attitude about getting to wherever she was going. She reminded me of an old trotter that can't slow down even though he's no longer in harness.

"It's a nice day, isn't it?" I said, taking off my suit jacket and draping it over my shoulder.

"Is it? I hadn't noticed," she said without breaking stride.

"Do you always walk this fast or are you in a hurry?"

"I always walk this fast. Though I can't see how that's any business of yours."

"Just making conversation," I said.

"Why?" she asked me. "Why waste my time and yours?"

"I need to talk to you."

"About what?"

"Your brother."

"My brother is dead."

I jumped over a crack to keep from breaking my mother's back. "That's news to me," I lied. "Who says so?"

"I say so," she replied, her speech as rapid-fire as her stride.

"Then how do you know?"

She stopped momentarily to glare at me. "I know, that's all. And I don't need for you to keep asking me how."

"All I'm after is some answers."

She started walking again. "I know what you're after. But you won't get it from me," she said. "You've met your match."

I saw trouble up ahead in the form of Stub Timmons. He was standing in front of his building. As we approached, he crossed Fair Haven Road and met us. "Is he troubling you again, Isabelle?" he said, blocking my path. "I told you before, Ryland. You're not wanted here."

Isabelle Glick glanced at him with what looked like revulsion. I glanced from one to the other, wondering what would happen next.

"You heard her, Ryland," Stub continued, interpreting Isabelle's silence for her. "Shove off."

He took a step toward me as if he meant business. I held my ground, though I doubted that I could take him one on one. He was about fifty pounds heavier and a lot stronger than I was. But I'd be damned if I'd back down from him, particularly in front of Isabelle Glick.

"Stub, please go on inside the house," Isabelle said. "I'll be there in a minute, as soon as Mr. Ryland and I are through talking."

155

Stub didn't protest as I expected him to, but went on inside her house.

"Why didn't you let Stub flatten me like he wanted to?" I asked.

"Because you amuse me," she said. "Because no one likes to guillotine the court jester. After all, what's the point?"

I could feel my ears burn. "Okay, I asked. You told me."

"Don't take it personally, my dear Garth," she said. "I like you. I always have." Her tone hardened. "It's just that you remind me too much of my dear departed brother."

"In what way?"

"His righteousness, which he substituted for his humanity." She stared at a nearby oak as if, given enough time, she could stare it down to the ground. "You see, most of us have little or no real humanity to begin with, only the pretense of it, which is usually enough to succeed in a gutless world. Today, all is appearances; it wasn't this way in the last century, and maybe not in the beginning of this one, but it surely is now." She turned her gaze on me. "And some of us, for whatever the reasons—and there are many—betray our humanity in the name of the very things we once fought so hard against. We betray it, for in the end we see the folly of maintaining it in a world that neither values nor appreciates it." She continued to stare at me. "And a precious few of us maintain our humanity to the end because we are either too blind or too weak or . . ." She looked away. It seemed to hurt her to continue. "Or perhaps because we are too innocent. I don't understand this innocence that defies logic and seems like blindness but isn't." She smiled grimly to herself. "Perhaps in the end we are all the same; our goodness or badness is in our blood, we don't choose it."

"I don't agree," I said. "If humanity and innocence

156

are at best an accident of birth, not something we have to earn and keep, then evil and inhumanity are also just an accident of birth. That makes it too easy to do, or be, whatever we happen to feel like doing or being, with no accounting for our actions."

"I don't care whether you agree or not," she said. "I didn't expect you to."

"And I don't agree with what you said about your brother," I continued. "You inferred that he had little or no humanity. I don't believe that. He seemed like a very humane man to me. Perhaps his fault, if you need one, wasn't a lack of humanity, but a misapplication of it. Perhaps he was never meant to be a judge."

"He wasn't meant to be a judge," she snapped. "Now are you through wasting my time?"

"Almost." I decided to quit playing her game, which I was no good at anyway, and go for all the marbles. If Sniffy Smith could somehow find the courage, so could I. "All I really need to know is, why did you kill your brother? Or did you have Stub Timmons do it for you?"

I didn't get the reaction I expected. Instead of denying it or evading it or laughing in my face as she had before, she said, "I had Stub do it for me, of course. He'll do anything I ask him to. He would even kill you if I'd like."

"I don't believe you," I said.

She was amused. In her presence I really did feel like the court jester. "What don't you believe? That I had Thorton killed, or that Stub would kill you if I asked him to?"

"That you had Thorton killed. Stub wouldn't need your permission to kill me, only the opportunity."

"Believe what you like," she said. "I can assure you that I'm capable of both." Then she squared her shoulders and marched into the house where Stub Timmons stood at the window watching us.

Early the next morning Rupert called me at the

157

Oakalla Reporter. His was the fifth call that I'd received since arriving at work, and none of them had been to compliment me on my fine work, so I wasn't in the best of moods when I answered the phone.

"*Oakalla Reporter.* Garth Ryland here."

"Garth, it's Rupert. You got a minute?"

"About that," I said. "What do you want?"

"If you're not interested, I won't bother you," he said with some bite in his voice.

"I'm interested. But this place won't run itself and lately that's what I've been asking it to do. What's on your mind?"

"It's not good news," he said. "That property over in the Barrens where you found the dump belongs to Judge Glick, or did before he died. It belongs to Isabelle Glick now."

"You're sure?" I felt as though he'd dropped a bomb on me. I didn't want to believe that Judge Glick would allow hazardous waste to be dumped on his property.

"I'm sure," he said. "I looked it up myself."

"In the City Building?"

"That's where the records are kept. What's your point, Garth?" He sounded impatient with me.

"I just wondered how you knew that Judge Glick's property in the Barrens now belongs to Isabelle Glick. Did you see a copy of his will?"

"Yes. I had to pull some rank and twist some arms, but I got a look at it a few minutes ago. The Judge left everything to Isabelle, except for his rare books, which he gave to the library, and his personal papers, which he left to someone that I'd never guess in a thousand years."

"Ruth?"

Silence from his end. I shouldn't have said anything. Somehow I had burst his bubble. "Sometimes I wonder why I even bother," he finally said.

158

"What were in his personal papers, do you know?" I wondered if something in them might point to the person who killed him.

But Rupert had lost interest, either in the papers or in our conversation, I wasn't sure which. "I don't know, Garth. I never got a good look at them. They're there in his desk at home, most of them anyway. If you're interested, you can take a look yourself."

"One last question," I said before he could hang up. "Does this mean you're back on the job again?"

"I'm not sure what it means," he said.

"Then what do you want to do with Judge Glick? We can't leave him in Doc Airhart's basement forever."

"I figure that's your problem, since you're the one who put him there."

"And what about the dump site? Are you going to clean it up or not?"

"I still haven't decided," he said. "The State Board of Health gave us until Friday to get our act cleaned up. If the water doesn't test any worse, I guess I can wait that long."

"Maybe I should be thankful for small favors," I said under my breath.

"What's that, Garth?" he asked.

"I said I wish to hell you'd get back on the job again. I'm tired of playing sheriff."

"I'll think about it," he said.

"While you're thinking about it, you might consider this," I said. "Isabelle Glick told me yesterday that she had Stub Timmons kill Judge Glick for her."

"Do you believe her?"

"I don't know what to believe, Rupert. She had plenty of reasons—jealousy, greed, revenge, hatred— reasons that have gotten a lot of people killed in the past and will be likely to in the future. But no, I don't believe her. Probably because I don't want to."

"Why don't you want to?"

I looked out at Gas Line Road where I saw the stranger's dark-blue 1955 Chevy drive by, pull into the park, and turn around. On his second pass he tooted. It sounded like good-bye to me. Without knowing why, I felt sad.

"Garth, you still there?" Rupert asked.

"I'm still here. What was your question again?"

"Why don't you want to think that Isabelle Glick had her brother killed?"

"Because I like her. And because I think life's dealt her a bum hand that most of us would have a hard time playing."

"That's not much to hang your hat on."

"No," I agreed. "It isn't."

After we hung up, I sat for several minutes thinking about the stranger. If he really was gone for good, I could breathe a huge sigh of relief. But at the same time I still had a lot of unanswered questions about him, such as who he was and what he was doing in Oakalla, and what he meant when he said that I wasn't in it for the money. So I really didn't know whether I was glad to see him go or not. Like Henry Higgins, I'd grown accustomed to his face.

I called Ruth. "No, I'm not going to do it, whatever it is," she said.

"Good morning to you too."

"What is it, Garth? And make it snappy because I've got a load of work to do today and was just about to get started."

"I just thought you might want to know before the fact that Judge Glick willed all of his personal papers to you. So if you don't want me to go through them before you do, you might want to stop by his house and pick them up."

"Thanks, but no thanks," she said. "If Thorton Glick had anything to say to me, he should have said it while he was alive when I had a chance to answer him."

Then she added, "I don't care much for hearing voices from the grave."

"Okay, but I gave you fair warning."

"And I'll give you fair warning. If you breathe a word of what's in those papers to another living soul, you'll be eating boiled turnips and stewed tomatoes for the rest of my life." She hung up.

I smiled as I put down the receiver. In boiled turnips and stewed tomatoes, she'd just issued the ultimate threat.

I deliberated a long time whether I should make a second phone call. In the end I decided not to make the call. Too much depended on Isabelle Glick's reaction, and while I wanted to trust her, I didn't completely. In her discussion about humanity, she'd never really said whether she'd kept hers or not. Too much was at stake for me to make a mistake about her.

•

15

A warm south wind had blown hard all day Wednesday, scattering the last of winter's debris and sending kites and birds soaring high into the air. I hadn't seen the stranger or his pickup since he'd driven by and honked on Monday morning, and the Corner Bar and Grill, which had begun to breathe a little easier on Monday and Tuesday, took a full deep breath on Wednesday as it celebrated his absence.

I couldn't say the same for me. Without him there to play the heavy, the Corner Bar and Grill had lost most of the drama that it had held in recent weeks. I ate supper there quickly and in silence, then returned to my office at the *Oakalla Reporter* where I sat bent over my typewriter with my hands raised and absolutely nothing of value to say. It was late into the night when I leaned back at my desk and ran my fingers along the smooth-as-glass blade of my knife. I let my thoughts wander.

I'd found a sheath for my knife among my boyhood treasures that I kept in my chest of drawers at home. The knife felt good there at my side. I liked knowing that it was with me, within reach, because I felt that I might need it once I went back into the cave again.

Clarkie parked his patrol car outside and came into

my office. Rupert had continued to stay at home while Clarkie continued to patrol the streets of Oakalla alone, confirming, by one misadventure after another, nearly everyone's entrenched opinion that he really didn't belong there without Rupert. But at the same time he also began to earn from even his harshest critics, Pete Hammond and Sniffy Smith among them, a grudging respect for his perseverance—though they'd never let Clarkie know that. He made too good a target for their jokes, the way things were.

"I'm not interrupting anything, am I, Garth?" Clarkie said. In the past, I'd have expected him merely to deliver a message from Rupert. Not today, though; he sat there with authority.

"Not that first thought, Clarkie. What's on your mind?"

"Is there anyone in town who owns a rust yellow El Camino besides Jimmy Parker?"

"Not that I know of. Why?"

"Because I could have sworn that I saw one parked in Rowena Parker's side yard when I was headed west along Jackson Street. But by the time I got turned around and drove back there, it was gone."

Without waiting for him to continue, I picked up the receiver and called Rowena Parker. She answered on the first ring. "Rowena, this is Garth Ryland. I know it's late and you were probably asleep, but will you do me a favor and check on Jimmy for me? It'll only take a minute."

"I just did a little while ago," she said. "In fact, I'd just gotten back into bed when you called. Jimmy's fine." I could hear another voice in the background. I assumed it belonged to David Roberts.

"Any particular reason why you checked on him when you did?" I asked.

The voice in the background grew louder. It didn't sound like a happy voice. "The neighbor's dog was

163

barking at something. So I got up to see what was the matter. Now I've got to go, Garth. Thanks for your concern." Someone slammed the receiver down. I was betting it wasn't Rowena.

"What was that all about?" Clarkie asked.

"Nothing apparently. Just a thought I had."

"It have anything to do with that yellow El Camino I thought I saw?"

"It has everything to do with it, Clarkie. If you're sure that's what you saw."

He put his hat back on and adjusted it to the way Rupert wore his. "I've been up since five this morning, Garth. But I think that's what I saw."

"Chances are that you did, then, Clarkie. Your eyes don't usually lie to you like they do to some people."

"I'm glad you noticed that I'm good for something." he said wearily. "That's more credit than I get from most of the folks around this town."

After Clarkie left, I mulled over what he'd seen and the implications that it had. Two thoughts came to me. The first said that the sooner I put Stub Timmons out of the salvage business the better. The second said that I no longer could delay entering the cave, no matter how much I wanted to.

A short while later a third thought came to me. It was time, I thought, for me and everyone else in Oakalla to give Clarkie his due.

The next morning Wilmer Wiemer put up a For Sale sign in Rowena Parker's front lawn. Ruth called me at the *Oakalla Reporter* to tell me. She also said that she'd seen an old dark-blue Chevy pickup parked beside the Corner Bar and Grill on her way uptown. She just wanted me to know in case I was interested.

With a spring in my step and a warm gale wind in my face, I walked uptown to the Corner Bar and Grill and saw Tom Two-Feathers' pickup parked outside. The stranger sat at his usual place at the counter.

164

But something had changed in his bearing. He sat straighter and taller than before. Like an old miner who had found the mother lode at last, he had a gleam of pure joy in his eyes that seemed to say, "Eureka! I have found it!"

I took a seat beside him and ordered Thursday's special, which was roast pork and dressing with mashed potatoes and applesauce on the side. Meanwhile, David Roberts came into the lunch room, took a seat in the first booth, and ordered a pitcher of beer. It seemed a little early in the day for David to be ordering beer by the pitcher, but if I read him right, he didn't care what time of day it was.

"You say something to me?" the stranger said.

"No. Not unless I was thinking out loud."

"My mistake."

"I was wondering what you were doing back here," I said. "I thought perhaps you'd gone."

He turned to look at me. I couldn't read his face, but his eyes had stopped smiling. "You mean you were hoping I'd gone," he said.

"That's not true," I said. "Actually I'm delighted to see you again."

He shrugged, turning away. "Then you're the only one."

It had never occurred to me that he might actually like the Corner Bar and Grill and its people, and that the reason he kept returning day after day was not to torment us with his presence but rather to enjoy whatever fellowship he might find there. "I'm sorry," I said. "I just assumed you were here for a reason, not because you particularly liked it here."

He took a drink of his coffee. "That's beside the point."

Bernice brought my dinner, along with a glass of milk. I glanced at David Roberts, who was almost at the

165

bottom of his first mug of beer and was in the process of pouring himself another glass.

"That looks like an unhappy young man over there, the stranger said. "I wonder what his problem is."

"Probably a woman," I guessed. "That's what always drove me to drink."

"Me too," he answered. "When I had one."

"You're not married anymore?"

That caught him off guard. "Who ever said I was married?"

"No one ever said," I replied. "I just assumed you had been."

"You're right. I was married," he answered. "My wife died a few years ago."

"What was her name?"

"Why?"

"Because I asked."

He retreated momentarily into the past, his eyes seemed to soften and turn inward. "Her name was Star Who Walks At Night. She was named after one of the Seven Sisters."

"Was she a Cheyenne?"

"No. She was a Blackfoot."

"I see," I said. "And her father was?"

"Tom Two-Feathers," he answered, and I felt that he was being truthful.

"And your name is?"

He wouldn't tell me. "That's not important. Now eat," he said gruffly. "Your dinner's getting cold."

We didn't speak the rest of the time that I sat at the counter. I finished my dinner, paid my bill, and stopped at David Roberts' booth on the way out. He'd finished the first pitcher of beer and started a second. By the time he finished the second pitcher he would be well on his way to wherever he wanted to go.

"You don't even need to ask," he said before I had a chance to say anything. "She kicked me out of her

166

house this morning and told me not to come back." He made a fist and punched the air viciously. "And all because of that little brat of hers. God, I hate that little sonofabitch."

"I take it you mean Jimmy."

"Who the hell else would I mean?" He downed a glass of beer and poured himself another one, spilling foam all over the table when he got the glass too full. "I can't stand the little wimp, and I don't care who knows it. He's just like his father, right down to his whiney little voice that just drives me up the wall." He chugged his glass of beer, but when he slammed it down to refill it, the glass scooted out of his hand and shattered on the floor. "Bernice, bring me another glass!" he yelled. When she didn't right away, he picked up the pitcher and began to drink out of it.

"Are you finished?" I asked.

"Finished with what, making a fool out of myself?" Leaning back in the booth, he reached into his shirt pocket and withdrew a pack of cigarettes. "It runs in the family, doesn't it?" he said, shaking a couple cigarettes out of the pack and lighting one of them. "Look at my old man. Now there's a fool for you. He gives this town his heart and soul and what does he get in return? A son like me. That's a laugh, isn't it, Garth? No matter what good he does for this town, I can undo it." Rupert suddenly entered the lunch room from the bar. David stood and gave him a mock salute. "Without even half trying."

I didn't remember when I'd last seen Rupert out in public without his uniform, but it shocked me to see him there in a work shirt and jeans. It shocked David as well when Rupert grabbed him by his arm and dragged him out of the booth. For a moment they stood toe to toe, as David dropped his cigarette and drew back his fist to swing. But he didn't swing on Rupert. Without any

167

apparent effort, he moved Rupert out of his way and left.

"You're not too careful about the company you keep, are you, Garth?" Rupert said.

"Are you going after him?" I asked.

He shook his head. "No. In my present frame of mind I'd probably do something that I'd regret later."

"Do you want me to go after him?"

"Do as you like, Garth. I'm going home." He gave the regulars of the Corner Bar and Grill a wave of apology and left.

I started to follow him out the door. "Ryland!" the stranger yelled at me. "Leave the man alone. The boy too. One doesn't need your help and the other won't take it, so you might as well save yourself the trouble."

"Is that the voice of experience talking?" I asked.

"That's an old man talking, who was once a young man." Ignoring the stare directed at him, he turned back to the counter.

I should have returned to the *Oakalla Reporter*, but instead I walked along Jackson Street to Rowena Parker's house. She normally would have had all her salon chairs filled at that time of day, but the blinds were down, and as far as I could tell, the beauty shop was empty. I knocked several times before she answered the door. When she finally did answer, I saw why she had been so slow in getting there. She wore a faded blue housecoat and no makeup, her hair limp and tangled, her eyes were red, and her nose ran. "Jimmy's not here," she said, wiping her nose with a Kleenex. "If that's who you're looking for. He's got kindergarten this afternoon."

"May I come in anyway?" I said. "I won't stay long."

She shook her head. "I'm really not dressed for company. Besides, we said about all there was to say a few nights ago."

168

"I see your house is up for sale. I wondered if that was before or after you had the fight with David."

A sudden strong wind nearly tore the door out of her grasp. She had to grab it in both hands and hold on. "Before. Though I don't see why that matters."

A stronger gust of wind pulled her out the door and down a step before she could regain her balance. I took hold of the door and together we nearly closed it again.

"I just saw David up at the Corner Bar and Grill," I said. "He's not doing so well either."

"Why should I care how he's doing?"

I shrugged. "I just thought you might. He didn't come back here by any chance, did he?"

"No," she said, fighting back the tears. "He didn't come back here."

"Well, in case he does, it might be a good idea to keep Jimmy away from him for a while. At least until he sobers up."

"He wouldn't hurt Jimmy," she insisted. "Drunk or sober."

I noted her puffed left cheek that appeared bruised and swollen. "It looks like he might have hurt you."

Instinctively she reached for her cheek. "I had it coming," she said. "I slapped him first."

"Why?"

"Because he called Jimmy a little bastard, just like his father." Her nostrils flared and her eyes momentarily came to life. "Well, he should know; David *is* Jimmy's father."

"Without a doubt?"

"Without a doubt. David left town, supposedly for good, just a few days before I found out that I was pregnant. I didn't start seeing Jimmy Parker until at least a month after that."

"Have you told David that?"

"No." She glared at me. "And don't you either."

"I won't. But why haven't you? It seems David has a right to know. I know that I would want to know if I had fathered a child. Particularly if I happened to love the child's mother, as David seems to love you."

She sighed, wrapping her housecoat more tightly around her. "I haven't told David that he's Jimmy's father because I want David to love me for my own sake, not because I'm the mother of his son."

"I can understand why you might want it that way," I said. "And ideally that's the way it should be. But you're not being fair to little Jimmy. Whether you've thought about it or not, you're demanding a second thing from David. You're asking the man to point blank love at first sight a child he thinks is another man's son. That's asking quite a lot of him. I know I couldn't do it. I'm not sure David can either. And little Jimmy's suffering in the process, missing the chance for love from his real father. I really think you'd both stand a lot better chance of getting through this if you told David the truth."

"Then I'd never know which of us he chose, me or Jimmy's mother," she said sadly.

"It's already obvious to me," I replied, "that he's chosen you. But you have to call it the way you see it."

"Thanks," she said. "I'll think about it."

I started to close the door. But then a thought occurred to me. "Does big Jimmy know who little Jimmy's father really is?"

When she hesitated to answer, I already knew what she was going to say. "Yes. I'm sorry to say he does. I vowed over and over again that I'd never tell him no matter how many times he asked. But once in a moment of anger, I threw it in his face," she said with regret. "I've never seen anyone look so devastated."

"Did that change his relationship with Jimmy in any way?"

"No. If anything it made him love Jimmy all the

170

more. Big Jimmy's not too proud of his own heritage anyway."

"Why not?"

"He's an orphan. He lived in several foster homes before he ended up in Oakalla. Even after he got here, he grew up pretty much on his own." She bit her lip. "That was one of the things that attracted me. His independence. And the way he seemed to care so much for me. But what I took for independence was really a lack of commitment. And what I took for caring was really a need to be cared for."

"Don't be too hard on yourself," I said. "We all make our share of mistakes along the way. I know I've made mine."

She gave me a smile, maybe her first that day. "It seems like I've heard that from you before, late at night up at the Corner Bar and Grill."

I smiled in return. "Well, even the best of us repeat ourselves."

She sighed, looking sad again. "Even our mistakes?"

"Particularly our mistakes."

"Thanks for nothing," she said. I pushed the door toward her. She took it in both hands and held on. "Garth," she said on my way down the steps. "What was the reason for your phone call late last night?"

"A false alarm," I said. "Why?"

"Because it started the fight that David and I had earlier today. I just hoped it was worth it."

"I'm sorry," I said. "But do me a favor, will you? Keep Jimmy's bedroom window locked."

"What good will that do?" she said. "He'll just unlock it again if he wants out."

"I wasn't thinking about little Jimmy."

"Who were you thinking about then? David?" She wouldn't let me finish. "When are you and the rest of this town going to give him a break and get off his case!"

She slammed the door before I could answer,

171

before I could tell her that I wasn't on David's case and that I had someone else in mind. I should have gone back up the steps and told her. But I didn't.

Hours later, with the *Oakalla Reporter* finally in bed and a stiff southwest wind still blowing, I walked up Gas Line Road and turned right at the cheese plant as if I were on my way home. But though I walked down the alley toward home, I didn't go home. I'd called Ruth earlier to tell her where I'd be and why. For once she didn't argue with me.

16

For the third straight day the wind was blowing, driving hard into the bricks and rattling the windows of Judge Glick's house. From my vantage point there in Judge Glick's bedroom, I could see Stub Timmons' building and driveway out the north window of the bedroom and his salvage yard out the west window. Evidently not an early riser, Stub had yet to make an appearance that morning. Nor had anyone stopped at his salvage yard for anything, at least not since dawn, which was when I'd started watching. I took a moment to study the second hand of my Timex to make sure it was moving. At eight-thirty A.M. it had already been a long day.

I had slept downstairs in the parlor of Judge Glick's house until first light, then I'd risen, drunk a cup of lukewarm coffee from my thermos, and watched the birds for a while. Because of the wind, they were unable to get a firm grasp on either the tree limbs or the light wires and spent most of their time shuttling back and forth between perches like commuters. That didn't include the robins, who spent most of their time on the ground, dodging sticks and grass straws while tiptoeing across the yard in a vain search for earthworms.

Stub's first customers arrived at exactly nine A.M.

riding in a new tan pickup with something covered by a tarpaulin in the bed. Stub came briefly out of his building to greet the two men in the cab before they all went inside. Moments later the two men emerged from the building and took off in the pickup, but not before I'd taken a photograph of them and their truck. An hour and a half after that, the same men in the same pickup returned. The driver got out of the cab, looked at his watch, and went on inside the building. I studied him through my telephoto lens: He looked relieved, like a man who'd just survived an audit by the I.R.S.

Stub reappeared at eleven with the arrival of another pickup, which also had a tarpaulin covering something in its bed. Gray, while the other was tan, this pickup also carried two men, who repeated the same procedure as the two men before them, arriving back at Stub's a few minutes before twelve-thirty P.M. Like the driver before him, the second driver also glanced at his watch on returning and wore a look of relief as he entered the building.

I reluctantly left my post at that point because Ruth and I had made a bargain: If I would scan Judge Glick's personal papers for her and remove for safekeeping anything that pointed in her direction, she would drive Jessie to the Marathon and fill her up for me. I had to start making good on my end of the bargain while I had the chance, and before another pickup arrived at Stub's.

I'd hurried across the bedroom to Judge Glick's desk and was just starting to search his papers when I heard his front door open and close. I hadn't seen Stub leave the building, so I didn't think it was him. But whoever it was must have had a key because the front door had been locked when I had checked it earlier that morning.

Without enough time to find a good place to hide, I chose the most obvious one and crawled under Judge Glick's four-poster bed. Just as I did, Isabelle Glick

174

entered the room, stood at the threshold momentarily as if unsure whether she was alone, then went quickly to Judge Glick's rare books and began to search through them.

A half hour passed. It sounded as though she was going through every book in Judge Glick's collection without finding what she was looking for. Her patience finally gave out, and I heard pages tear and spines crack as she began to rifle through the books and slam them back into place. Her rage grew even more frenzied until, in a final act of frustration, she tore books from the shelves and flung them about the room.

Then she leaned against her brother's desk and cried, "What has changed, Thorton? Even in death you better me. You who were so pious, so proper, so *respected* could afford to be. You had no soul to lose. Whereas I did. So now you've become the martyr and I've become your executioner. Isn't that ironic, Thorton? Wouldn't Father just die!"

Stumbling blindly about his room, she threw whatever she could get her hands on. When she came to his closet, she began to rip apart his clothes. But suddenly she stopped her rampage, clutched something in her arms, pulled it down to the floor with her, and began to sob. "Goddamn you, Thorton," she said. "*I* should have been the judge." I couldn't see well enough to be sure, but the black cloth clutched in her arms looked like a judge's robe. Then she rose and left, taking the robe with her.

For a moment, I was too stunned to move. Then I crawled out from under the bed and stood. Minutes passed. I listened to the wind buffet the house with gust after gust that seemed to shake its very foundation. I momentarily forgot Stub Timmons and his customers and why I'd gone to Judge Glick's in the first place. Isabelle Glick had made me forget.

I spent the next four hours alternating between

175

watching at the window and going through Judge Glick's personal papers. As the afternoon wore on, I wished I had brought something along to eat. Even Ruth's tuna casserole would have tasted good by then.

Stub's last customers arrived at five, left shortly thereafter in a shiny black pickup to drive north on Fair Haven Road, and returned about an hour and a half later to complete the same ritual as the others. Stub came outside, waited for them to clear the drive, then took a long look in all directions before he went around back to his salvage yard. There he produced a set of keys from his pocket and unlocked the trunk of what appeared to be an old two-tone, turquoise-and-white Buick Roadmaster. Then he took a suitcase out of the trunk of the Buick and put something into it. I had a guess of what that something might be, but by then it was nearly too dark for me to see.

Stub went immediately to his white pickup and drove north on Fair Haven Road. I hadn't anticipated that move and wasn't ready for it. If Ruth had kept her part of the bargain as I had mine, Jessie waited for me at home with a full tank of gas. But if Stub was headed where I hoped he was, I didn't have time to go home after her. That left me with no other choice. I took Judge Glick's gold Cadillac.

17

I first saw the lights of the car following me when I turned right at the junction of Fair Haven Road and Haggerty Lane. The car stayed a steady distance behind me, just far enough away so that I couldn't see who it was, yet close enough to keep me in sight. I sped up. It sped up. I slowed down. It slowed down. I pulled into a farmer's lane and shut off my lights. It waited for me to turn them on and take off again. Then I lost it. Or it lost me. One minute it was behind me and the next minute it wasn't. Driving slowly without my lights, I thought I'd surely see it again, but I didn't. I felt uneasy about that. Alone, out in the Barrens, I couldn't afford too many surprises.

Leaving Judge Glick's Cadillac parked in a pine thicket next to the gravel road, I walked the last quarter mile of my journey. I had hoped the wind would die at dusk, as it did sometimes after blowing hard all day. But nightfall only seemed to magnify its intensity; it rose to an incessant wail that sometimes became a howl and stayed there. I tried to walk backward into it but had no success. Heavy and tireless, it kept hammering away at me until I had to turn around and lean into it if I wanted to get anywhere. A grit that must have come all the way from west Texas stuffed my nose and made my teeth squeak whenever I bit down. "A night not fit for man or beast," Grandmother Ryland would have said.

Nothing seemed to be moving inside the sheet-metal building there in the Barrens. For an unhappy moment I thought I'd mistaken Stub's intentions and outsmarted myself. He had probably made a circle and gone back to the Corner Bar and Grill to play euchre. Either that or he'd somehow caught wind of what I was doing and decided to follow me, instead of the other way around.

I had wondered what Judge Glick had seen out of his bedroom window that seemed unusual enough for him to write it down. He'd seen arrivals and then departures every two hours by the same vehicles at the same time throughout each week. Then he'd probably listed the license plate numbers of the vehicles, or had them checked out in some other way to see who owned them. In doing so, he must have discovered that all of the businesses whose trucks regularly came to Stub's salvage yard also employed Isabelle Glick as their accountant. Timing the trucks from when they left Stub's until they returned, he knew approximately how far they'd gone; he also knew that the land he owned in the Barrens fell within that radius. So he went out to see for himself and found the same dump where I had found him dead in a blue barrel five years later. Had he then in a righteous rage kicked Isabelle out of his house and resigned from the bench because he no longer felt morally fit to pass judgment? I didn't know for sure, but I guessed that was what had happened.

Someone turned on a light inside the building. If it was Stub, and I was almost certain that it was, where had he parked his white pickup and why had it taken him so long to turn on the light? For some reason, perhaps because of the wind, he seemed to be moving more cautiously and deliberately than usual.

178

The gate into the building stood partially open. I went inside the gate and discovered that Stub's white pickup was parked in a shadow along the west side of the building. Approaching the large sliding door that opened into the building itself, I noticed that while the door was nearly wide open, the light inside had gone off. I looked and listened for something to tell me where he was, but I could hear only the wind.

I went back around to the west side of the building and took a photograph of Stub's pickup, another photograph of the building itself, and a third of Stub's truck, license plate, and building all in the same frame. These, along with the other photographs that I'd taken of the company trucks and drivers earlier in the day, probably gave me enough ammunition to put Stub and his customers out of the hazardous waste business. All I had to do was show them the photographs and threaten to print them in the *Oakalla Reporter* if they didn't stop. But I didn't have enough evidence to send Stub to jail and that was what I wanted most. Everything else aside, I didn't like Stub Timmons, and that was that. No use in pretending otherwise.

I approached the building, which reverberated in the wind like a huge metal drum. When I didn't see any sign of Stub inside, I should have stopped there, taken my half loaf, and gone home. Instead, I went into the building.

Something warned me an instant before Stub swung or I would have been a dead Garth. He swung at my head with a lead pipe that he must have kept there in the building just for the purpose of bashing heads. KEEP OUT! *This means you. If you think I'm kidding, come on in!!* He wasn't kidding. I ducked just in time and the pipe slammed into the side of the building with a thud.

Then the lights came on. Stub stood there like a batter about to lay down a bunt. He crouched between me and the door with the pipe held in both hands in

179

front of him. All of the meanness I'd glimpsed in him over the years, all of the savagery that I'd felt and responded to in kind, was there in his face for me to see. There was no mistaking his intent. He planned to kill me.

"You don't know how I've waited for this, Ryland," he said as a smile appeared momentarily, then disappeared just as quickly. "You just don't know."

"I think I can guess," I said, taking a step backward to counter the step he took forward. "I could say it's nothing personal. But I'd be a liar." I smiled at him, trying to slow him down a little. "I know my reasons. But what are yours?"

He took one more step toward me, then stopped to think about what I'd asked him; for Stub, a man of instinct and emotion, this took effort, but not as much as I had hoped. "That's easy enough to answer," he said. "For eight years now you've been telling Oakalla what to do and how to think. No, you don't come right out and say it, but it's there in your writing. I had a good business until you came to town, doing a little favor here, another favor there, skimming a little of the cream off the top for myself, but not so much as to kill the cow. But things began to tighten up after you came and started poking your nose into other people's business, all the while preaching at us in that column of yours. People either got nervous or got conscience, one or the other, but both bad for me. So I had to dig a little deeper just to get by."

"I'm an annoyance, is that it?" If I could keep him talking, at least he wouldn't be swinging his lead pipe at me.

"Among other things," he said, taking a step to stay between me and the door. "But that's not all, Ryland. Besides being a royal pain in the ass, you're a moralist, or whatever they call those people who have opinions about the way things ought to be." He began to shift the

180

lead pipe back and forth between his hands. "That wouldn't be so bad, except none of your so-called morals include me, or my kind. So the way I see it, that makes you the enemy."

"One man's poison . . ." I said, "is another man's meat. But that's the hazard when we all drink from the same river."

"What the hell are you talking about, Ryland?"

"Life, Stub. We seem to be at opposite ends of it."

"So what are you going to do about it?" he said with a smile. "This is one time you can't write your way out of it."

"If you had a typewriter, I could try."

"Ha! Very funny. But as you can see, I'm not laughing." Taking another short step, he tried to cut down the distance between us and at the same time improve his angle. "So you might as well give me that camera you're carrying, unless you want it all busted up, like you're about to be."

That sounded like a good idea to me, so I took my camera off my shoulder and threw it at him. He swung at it, but missed. Unfortunately I also missed my mark, which was Stubb's head.

"Strike one," I said.

I took the quartz knife from its sheath on my belt.

Stub hadn't counted on my being armed. I could see the look of surprise on his face. "That knife doesn't change anything," he said.

I held the knife out in front of me so that he could watch it gleam in the light. "I think it does. It's the same knife that killed Judge Glick, you know."

Stub stopped dead in his tracks. "That's a lie. You didn't kill Judge Glick."

"Neither did you, Stub. You found him here and stuffed him into an empty barrel, then sealed the cave, but you didn't kill him."

"Just what are you saying, Ryland?" He began to

move again, but with less certainty than before. Apparently I'd spoken the truth.

"I'm saying it doesn't have to come to this, Stub. I know you want to kill me, but I don't necessarily want to kill you." Then I said in all sincerity, "But I will kill you, Stub, if you leave me no other choice."

"You don't scare me, Ryland. Neither does that puny little knife you're carrying." He'd set himself to take a swing at me. I kept my eyes concentrated on his hands, because the swing would start from there.

"The knife's magical, Stub, at least five hundred years old and made by the greatest warrior who ever lived in Wisconsin. It's a scalping knife, Stub. I wonder what yours will look like hanging from my belt."

Stub swung at me, missed as I jumped backward, and left himself open. But I decided to go for the door instead of Stub, and would have made it easily had he not continued on around with his swing, caught my left ankle, and tripped me. That hurt. Tears welled up in my eyes as I rolled to a crouch, facing him. The door was behind me. All I had to do was back out of it and take off. But there was the camera to think about. Maybe my wanting that film held me there. Or maybe I just wanted to have it out with Stub at last. Either way, I stayed.

"It's your move, Stub," I said as I started toward him with the knife pointed at his belly.

"I got you once. I can get you again." But he began to backpedal. He'd lost some of his confidence.

"Think about it, Stub, how ugly your bare scalp's going to look hanging there. Now if you just had a head of thick white hair like Judge Glick . . ."

"Shut up!" he yelled. "Shut the hell up!"

I didn't have a plan. Maybe I could eventually back him over a barrel, but I didn't think so. My only thought was to goad him as much as possible, make him so scared or angry that he'd get careless.

182

But Stub might also stop backpedaling and set his feet to swing, and then he might have the advantage. So when he glanced behind him to see what might be there, I charged, butting him in the face with the top of my head. The collision momentarily stunned both of us as he fell backward on the concrete floor and I fell on top of him. Rolling away to escape his powerful arms, I heard him bellow like a bull at the same time I saw the blood spurt from his nose. I knew what was going to happen next, so before it did, I grabbed my camera from the floor and headed for the door.

Enraged and half blinded by his own blood, Stub swung at the first thing he came to, but hit a barrel instead of me. When a second barrel got in his way, he swung at that too, and then at one of the steel pillars that supported the building. Finally he got a fix on me just as I was leaving and blindly charged the door.

What he didn't know was that I didn't leave. I darted silently to the side and waited until he was almost to the opening before I slid the door closed. He hit it full force and dropped to his knees. Before he could rise, I swung around behind him and put the knife to his throat. At the same instant someone shined a flashlight in my eyes.

"That'll probably be enough, Garth," Rupert said. "I think Stub's had all he wants for one night."

But I didn't move. It was almost as if the knife in my hand wouldn't let me move. It wanted to taste Stub for itself.

"I said that'll be enough, Garth," Rupert repeated forcefully. "Don't do what you're about to."

I let go of Stub and sheathed the knife.

While Stub was still on his knees, Rupert put a pair of handcuffs on him and read him his rights. "It's okay, Clarkie," Rupert said. "You can come out now."

I didn't know which scared me more, seeing Stub Timmons with a lead pipe in his hands, or seeing

Clarkie holding a loaded revolver. He kept it pointed at Stub the whole time that Rupert and I were helping him to his feet. Then Stub made a sudden move trying to shake himself free, I heard Clarkie's hammer click, I thought for sure Stub had bought the farm.

"Easy, Clarkie," Rupert said slowly, and I could see that he was ready to deflect Clarkie's aim. "He's not going anywhere."

Clarkie eased the hammer down and put his revolver back into his holster. "Not if I have anything to say about it." But when Clarkie tried to lead Stub away to his patrol car, Stub shook him off like a leaf that had fallen on to his shoulder.

"Get your hands off of me," Stub growled. "You little pimp." Then he turned back to Rupert. "You ain't getting nothing from me until I talk to my lawyer." His eyes found mine. They said how much he hated me. "And I'll see you later."

I held up my camera. "I'm sure you will, Stub."

"Bastard!" he yelled at me, just before Clarkie gave him a shove in the direction of the patrol car.

"Pimp yourself," Clarkie said, dodging Stub's foot.

I took a quick look at my camera. The lens was broken, but other than that it seemed to be okay.

"When you get that fixed," Rupert said, "be sure to send me the bill."

"You can count on it."

We went back inside the building where Stub's lead pipe lay beside a smear of his blood on the floor. I took a long look at it, remembering the sound as it whizzed past my head and the feel of it as it clipped my ankle. If it had hit full force, things might have turned out differently.

"What took you so long?" I asked. I guessed that Rupert and Clarkie were the ones who'd followed me from Oakalla.

"Clarkie," Rupert said, pinching off a chew of

tobacco and putting it into his mouth. "He said he knew a shortcut and got us lost."

"At least you got here," I said.

He put a firm clasp on my shoulder. It told me he was all the way back to being sheriff again. "That we did."

Together we walked to the back of the building where the barrels were stacked one upon the other as high as Stub could pile them with his forklift. Five barrels, apparently that day's collection, stood in a row, waiting to be stacked. Rupert looked at them in disgust, then spat on the nearest one. "Where's the other dump, the one that's poisoning the water?"

"Out back. I'll show you in a minute."

"You can show me tomorrow," he said. "I'll need to come back and take pictures anyway, along with bringing along somebody in the know, I reckon."

"Is that wise?" I asked. "You know what'll happen once somebody from the outside gets ahold of this. They'll come in here with their guns loaded and shoot the first thing that moves, which will probably be our water supply."

He spat again, hitting the barrel squarely in the middle. "I know that better than you do, Garth. I've been dealing with bureaucrats in one form or another for most of my life, which is why I wanted this job, to get away from them. But I don't see how we can get around it. We can't afford to clean up this mess ourselves."

"What if we could afford it?" I asked.

He brightened at the thought. "Then I'd do everything in my power to see that we cleaned it up ourselves."

"It's a deal," I said. "Check back with me the first chance you get."

"I suppose there's no use asking where the money's coming from."

"An anonymous donor" was all I would say.

A particularly fierce gust of wind shook the whole building and threatened to take the roof off. Rupert and I shared a look, then we walked toward the door.

"How did Stub have it set up," he asked, "to even get this far with it?"

"I'm not sure Stub set it up," I said, thinking about Isabelle Glick. "But Stub did run the nuts and bolts of the operation, which revolved around a time clock that Stub has in his building back in Oakalla, and a two-hour delivery schedule every Wednesday and Friday."

"Are you saying Stub clocked them in and out?" he asked.

"It stands to reason. He wouldn't want two deliveries to arrive at the same time. That would only complicate matters. And he wouldn't want whoever was making the delivery out here to take too long about it. Otherwise, they might have another truck waiting somewhere and slip in an extra barrel or two. So by keeping them on a tight schedule, he kept them honest." I had to smile. "So to speak."

"But where did the deliveries come from?" he asked. "There are only a few companies around Oakalla, and they've always played by the rules as far as I know."

"Not all of them, Rupert," I said sadly, remembering some of the names on Judge Glick's list. "Not all of them."

"You still haven't answered my question," he pointed out. "Where did the deliveries come from?"

"Here, there, and everywhere," I said. "Some from as far away as Madison. At least two of the trucks that delivered to Stub today had Dane County license plates."

"All of them small companies?"

"That'd be my guess, yes. They probably didn't think they could afford what it would have cost them to dispose of their toxic waste legally. So they came to Stub."

"On whose recommendation?"

I hesitated to tell him. I wanted to deal with Isabelle Glick myself and at least hear her side of the story. "Can that wait until tomorrow?"

"Yes," he answered. Then he said in a voice that left no doubt, "But no longer."

Remembering the look of relief on each driver's face as he arrived back at Stub's, I said, "It'd also be my guess Stub had some kind of fine set up in case they didn't get back from here in time. And one key that he sent out with each driver."

"When did Stub get paid?" Rupert asked.

"Probably when they arrived. Knowing Stub, he'd want to see the color of their money before he ever handed over the key."

"Knowing Stub," Rupert agreed.

Outside, the wind met us with a roar, nearly escaping with Rupert's hat before he could corral it. "You want a ride back to the Judge's car?" he asked, holding down his hat with both hands.

"No," I shouted. "The way my ankle feels, the walk will do me good."

"See you back in Oakalla then."

"Rupert?" I asked before I left. "How did you know to follow me? Did Ruth put you up to it?"

"No," he answered. "I figured it out myself." He smiled. "What do you think about that?"

"I think I'm glad you did. Where were you all day?"

"At Edgar Shoemaker's, drinking coffee and swapping stories with Edgar." He winked at me. "You might try it sometime. It's a great place to kill time."

"I'll remember that. Where was Clarkie while you were there?"

He glanced in the direction of the patrol car where

187

Clarkie and Stub Timmons sat waiting for him. "Wherever I needed him to be."

"I still think he's underpaid."

Rupert spat with the wind for what must have been a world's record. "So does he. Thanks to you."

"He read you the articles I wrote on him, huh?"

"He not only read it," Rupert said with disgust. "He taped it to his dashboard." He turned toward the patrol car. "Right in front of where I have to sit."

I waited until they all left before starting the walk back to Judge Glick's car. With the wind at my back, I made good time. Then I felt the presence of something very close behind me. Without a backward glance, I climbed into the Cadillac, fumbled with the keys momentarily before I found the ignition, and drove away.

"Just my imagination playing tricks on me," I said aloud to reassure myself. But I knew better.

18

Isabelle Glick had her porch light on. I knocked and then waited there on the porch in the wind, though I doubted that she could have heard me. "Isabelle!" I yelled. "Are you there?" When no one answered, I opened the door and went inside.

She sat in the middle of the living room in a chair facing me. One bare bright light bulb burned overhead, directly above her. She had cut off most of her hair and wore her brother's black robe. I was amazed at how closely they resembled each other. For a moment, before my eyes adjusted to the light, I thought that it was Thorton sitting there.

"Court is now in session," she said solemnly. "The people of Oakalla, Wisconsin, versus Isabelle Glick." She turned to look my way. She seemed to have been expecting me. "And how do you plead, Isabelle Glick, guilty or not guilty?" Before I could answer, she continued. "Perhaps you would like to hear the charges leveled against you. Would you, Isabelle?"

I didn't know whether I should answer. "Yes," I said.

"Why?" she asked. "Do you think you're guilty?"

"I don't know," I said. "Am I?"

She rose from her chair and began to stalk stiffly about the room. Then I noticed another presence in the room, that of her father. He stared sternly down at her from his portrait, as if he were about to pass judgment on her. And I feared that his verdict would be harsher than mine.

"Guilt presumes innocence," Isabelle said. "It is the law of two contraries, equal and opposite forces, and without one we cannot have the other; just as we cannot have courage without first knowing fear. If I am to judge you, Isabelle, I must first know your intentions. In the beginning, did you start out to poison the waters of Oakalla?"

"No." I hoped that I was answering truthfully for her.

"Then what did you start out to do?"

"I started out to be the best woman I possibly could."

"And were you?"

"Yes. Without question."

She stopped pacing and stood before me with all of her weight resting on her front foot, like a giant black crane about to spear a fish. "And what did that earn you, Isabelle?"

"Fear . . ." Then I felt compelled to add, "And respect."

She rocked forward, as if propelled by the gust of wind that shook the house. "Liar! No one respected you, Isabelle Glick. They feared you and your knowledge, that's all."

"I did," I said.

She wore a smile of contempt. "Did you really?"

I tried to hold her gaze, but couldn't, and had to look away.

"So, Isabelle," she said, clapping her hands once to break the spell before she began to pace about the room once more. "What else besides fear did all of your good

190

intentions earn you?" When I didn't answer, she answered for me. "Money perhaps?"

I shrugged. "Some. Enough to buy some of the things I wanted."

"Such as?" She prompted me.

"Furs and clothes, a few nice pieces of jewelry."

"Did you look good in them?" she stopped her pacing to ask.

"Stunning. I was the envy of every woman in Oakalla."

Pleased with my answer, she smiled and clapped her hands, then began to pace again. "What else, Isabelle? What else?"

Stretching my mind to try to match hers, I said, "Position. And power. I was queen of Oakalla for most of the time that my brother was king."

"I was still second to my brother, King Thorton," she said bitterly. "First, last, and always. No matter who I was or what I did, he was always first." She turned to look at the portrait behind her, "Wasn't he, Father?"

I thought about the last time I'd seen Thorton Glick in public. Dressed in full regalia that included an all-red riding outfit, silver stirrups, and a silver-studded saddle, he rode a white Arabian at the head of Oakalla's homecoming parade. On that day, as on all others, he pranced through the streets of Oakalla, waving to all of his admirers; he could do no wrong in our eyes. Perhaps that was the way it had always been, even at home.

Silence overtook the room as the wind drowned out everything but itself. Twice the bulb overhead flickered as power lines rubbed together in the wind, but the light did not go out. I sat and waited for her to continue.

"I'm not through with you yet, Isabelle," she said dully, leaving the window.

"I know."

She returned to her seat under the bare bulb, which cast a black shadow across one side of her face, leaving

191

the other side white. "You still haven't answered the final question, Isabelle," she said. "Why did you, in spite of everything, decide to do what you did?"

I took my time in answering because I didn't know the answer. "I think you ask too much of me," I said. "No one knows himself that well."

"You do, Isabelle," she said with certainty. "So please answer the question."

"And if I can't?"

Her eyes never wavered, never considered asking for mercy or granting it. "Then I must find you guilty and sentence you to death." She withdrew a small pistol from the pocket of her robe and laid it in her lap.

"The punishment must fit the crime," I said.

"It will."

In the silence that followed,the wind never once let up as it whipped the trees until it seemed that one of them would surely be uprooted. Twice more the bulb flickered, and each time I leaned forward, awaiting my chance to take the pistol from Isabelle Glick, but both times that chance was denied. I felt that if I answered truthfully she might kill herself. But if I lied, she might kill me.

"I'm sorry," I said. "I won't answer. The stakes are too high."

"Your life, you mean."

"And yours."

I waited for her to speak. Finally she did.

"My motive?" she began. "My motive is as old as man himself. Greed. I saw myself in my old age, living off my social security, or Thorton's charity, which would have been infinitely worse. Yes, I did have some money set aside, but not enough to last me as long as I planned to live, which was one breath longer than my brother. And the reason for this," she said, as her robed arm swept the room like a black wing, "the reason I have lived in such poverty, such *squalor* . . ."—her face re-

192

vealed just how much she hated that house—"is that Thorton, who by then knew that it was too late to stop me, threatened to expose me if I spent one dime of the money I'd earned from my enterprise with Stub." One turquoise eye showed clearly in the bright light, while the other was dimmed by shadows. "So everything that Stub and I have earned together is hidden where you, and no one else in this town, will ever find it." Then she picked up the pistol and pointed it at me. "So, now that you know the truth, and not your poor romantic notion of it, what do you plan to do with me?" The look in her eye gave me a pretty good idea of what she planned to do, which was to shoot me.

"There's nothing to do to you," I answered calmly, rising from the chair. "You've already done it to yourself."

"Where are you going?" she demanded.

"Home. It's been a long day."

"No, you are not!" she said, her voice shrill. "I'll shoot you first. I swear I will."

I turned to face her. I had no trouble at all holding her gaze then. "No, you won't shoot me, Isabelle. Because I'm not the one who's guilty. You are." I pointed to the portrait of her father. "Ask him and everything he stood for. Ask your brother, who even though he was in your eyes a weak man was still a good man to the very end, who even though he was crippled by a stroke went into a cave looking for Jimmy Parker and got himself killed in the bargain. Then ask yourself why, since you've known of your brother's death for nearly two weeks now, why you still haven't spent a dime of that money. You can't, Isabelle. You never will. You'll never escape your own conscience, your own rock-ribbed love of goodness and honor that has always been a part of you. Why, Isabelle? Because it's in your blood. As surely as a thoroughbred is born to race, you were born to do good."

"I was born to *judge!*" she cried.

"Then judge me. I'm leaving."

I turned and left, fully expecting to be shot in the back before I ever reached the door. When that didn't happen, I closed the door behind me and started walking home. The wind continued to blow. I never heard the shot that killed Isabelle Glick.

19

I walked through my back door just in time to hear the phone ring. Ruth beat me to it by a step. "If it's anybody but Rupert, I'm not here," I said. A moment later she handed me the receiver. "Yes, Rupert."

"You don't sound quite yourself," he observed. "Did I get you out of bed?"

"No. I just came in the door."

"From where?"

"I'll tell you about it later. What's the problem?"

"I just got a call from Sadie Jenkins," he said. "She can't be sure because of the wind, but she thought she heard an explosion a while back over at Jimmy Parker's."

"Why don't you pick me up on your way there."

"I planned to."

As I handed the receiver back to her, Ruth said, "Want to tell me about it?"

I told her what Rupert had told me.

She took her seat at the kitchen table and kicked out my chair so that I could sit down. "I mean where you've been for the last twenty-four hours. You look like something the cat dragged in."

195

I took my seat across from her and rubbed the back of my neck, trying to get my headache to go away. I hadn't eaten in so long that I wondered what food tasted like. What I'd been planning on when I got home was a tall highball, a big bowl of popcorn, and then a steaming hot shower before bed. The last thing I wanted to do was to go out again that night.

"I just came from Isabelle Glick's," I said. "And the Barrens before that. All in all, I've spent more relaxed evenings."

"Why? What happened?"

I told her as best I could in the few minutes that I had before Rupert got there. "The worst part of it," I said, "is that I liked Isabelle Glick. I still do for that matter."

"Are you going to tell Rupert what you know about her? He'll want to know, I'm sure."

I smiled at her perception. "He's already told me as much. But I don't know, Ruth. I have to think on it." Then I remembered that Isabelle Glick still held a loaded pistol when I left her. With her, anything was possible. "It might not matter anyway," I said. I told her why.

She frowned and leaned back in her chair. "Then why did she bother to write you that letter eight years ago about the hazardous waste, if she knew that was the direction she was headed anyway?"

"I don't think she wrote it, Ruth. I think her brother did. He knew what was going on with Stub, even though he didn't yet know Isabelle was involved with it. My guess is that she wasn't at that time. Judge Glick told her about it and she took it from there, making the contact with Stub, perhaps threatening to expose him if he didn't cut her in. From there on they gradually expanded and refined their operation as they went along."

"Two peas in a pod," Ruth said in disgust.

"It appears so."

"But then why did Thorton write that letter to you, instead of exposing Stub himself? And why did he say those terrible things about himself?"

Seeing Rupert's patrol car pull up outside, I rose from the table. "I can only guess why he called himself what he did," I said. "Maybe he truly felt it. You have to remember where he was in his life and the fact that you knocked the props out from under him not too long before that. Or maybe he wanted to disguise his own hand in the matter and that was the best way to do it." Rupert tooted his horn. I could barely hear it above the wind. "As for why he didn't turn Stub in himself, I'll leave that to you to answer. Why won't you believe that Stub killed Judge Glick? We both know he's capable of it. And as I recall, you've never been too fond of Stub Timmons either."

"I'm not," she answered. "And I'll be the first to tell you that. Stub's worth just about as much on this earth as jimson weed. Which is to say he's worthless. But he and Thorton were neighbors, living side by side here in Oakalla for most of their lives. I'd like to think that meant something, even to Stub."

"I'd like to think that meant something to Thorton too," I said.

The wind nearly ripped the storm door out of my hand on my way outside. Rupert waited for me in his patrol car. He had an unusually solemn look on his face.

"What's the problem?" I asked.

"I got another phone call just before I left. It seems that little Jimmy Parker has disappeared again."

"When?"

He shook his head. "That's all I know. His mother was too upset to talk. I'm on my way there now."

Rowena Parker wore a look of utter despair. She sat on the edge of her couch, walking her fingers nervously up and down the front of her housecoat. She'd brushed her hair since the last time I'd seen her and put on some makeup that left her lips redder and fuller, and her already dark eyes darker. But she seemed not to care how she looked; I saw on her face only one thing— concern for her missing son.

"Tell me again what happened, Mrs. Parker," Rupert said.

"Please don't call me that," she replied. "I hate to be called that."

"Just tell me what happened then," Rupert said, starting to lose patience with her.

"I don't know what happened!" she said, hugging herself. "David said he thought he heard a noise and went to investigate. When he didn't come back to the bedroom, I called to him, but he didn't answer. So I went looking for him and found the door to Jimmy's bedroom open. So was Jimmy's window . . ."

"But no Jimmy or David," I said when she didn't continue.

She shivered, clutching herself ever tighter. "No. They were both gone."

"Was the window locked, Mrs.—" Rupert caught himself. "Was the window locked?"

"No. Yes . . . I don't know!" she stammered. "Why does that matter anyway?"

Rupert looked at me as if to say that it was my turn. "It matters," I said, "because whoever took Jimmy should have had to come from the outside in to get him. But if the window and all of the doors were locked . . . well, you see the problem."

That angered her. "So you think David took him, right? Why couldn't Jimmy have climbed out the window like he did before?"

"He could have," I said. "But I don't think he did. Neither do you." Seeing the fear in her eyes, I added, "Or have I read you wrong?"

She pressed her hand to her mouth to keep from

198

crying. "It wasn't David," she insisted. "I know it wasn't."

"How long was David gone before you went looking for him?" Rupert asked.

She shook her head. "I don't know. A few minutes, maybe longer. I might have gone back to sleep. I can't say."

"Did you hear the noise that David thought he heard?" Rupert persisted.

"No," she said. "But David is a much lighter sleeper than I am. He hears everything that goes on."

"Even in this wind?" Rupert said.

"He's your son!" Rowena exploded. "How can you even think what you're thinking?"

"Because I've known him a lot longer than you have," Rupert calmly answered. "I've known him longer than you've even been alive."

"Which makes him capable of what?" she asked, her eyes flashing. "Answer me, Sheriff Roberts. As a father, and not because of the badge you're wearing."

"I answered you as a father," he replied. "Every time I think David has sunk as low as he can get, he finds a way to prove me wrong. I used to think my son had limits, Mrs. Parker, beyond which even he wouldn't go. But I have yet to find them. Have you?"

She wouldn't look at him, choosing to look at the floor instead. "I asked you not to call me that," she said. "My name is not Mrs. Parker. It is Rowena *Roberts*." She raised her head defiantly. "Did you hear me? My name is Rowena *Roberts*. David and I were married today."

Rupert put on his hat and rose from the couch.

"Rupert, while we're here, maybe we'd better take a look at Jimmy's bedroom," I said. After the way Rowena had defended him, David deserved at least that much from us.

"What's the point, Garth?" he asked.

"Rotten eggs," I said. "Don't you smell them?"

"That's all I have smelled for the past month," he

199

said wearily as his eyes swept the room. "It seems I can't get away from it."

"Listen then," I said. "Do you hear any water running?"

"No," he admitted. "I don't."

"Then where is the smell coming from?"

We went to Jimmy's room. As we entered, a gust of wind rushed in from outside, billowing the curtains and scattering Jimmy's coloring book and crayons all over the floor. In the bedroom itself the smell of rotten eggs had begun to fade as the wind spread it throughout the house. But a pocket of it still lingered in Jimmy's closet and led me to believe that the smell had originated there.

"Mickey's here," I said to Rupert.

"Who's Mickey?"

I picked up Jimmy's stuffed dog from the floor to show him.

Rupert didn't see my point. "So what?" he asked. "We're looking for the boy, not his stuffed dog."

"If Jimmy had run away, Mickey would be with him."

Rupert gave me a strange look. "Then that means David took him."

"Not David," I said. At least I didn't think that it was David.

"Who then?"

I told him. Rupert rushed from the house with me at his heels.

We found David Roberts in the alley behind Rowena's house. He had a deep gash in his throat, but he was conscious, and seemed alert, even though he made no attempt to move. While Rupert went after Rowena and his patrol car, I held David's head up so that he wouldn't choke on his own blood.

"Evening, Garth," he said calmly, looking up at the stars.

200

"Evening, David," I replied, as a gust of wind swirled down the alley, showering us with dust. "You picked a hell of a night to take a walk."

"I pick a hell of a night to do everything, it seems," he answered.

"Did you get a chance to see who attacked you?"

"No. He came at me from behind. Before I knew it he was gone." I waited for him to get his breath. "How's Rowena? She's not hurt, is she?"

"She's fine. She said you two got married today."

He smiled. "She never could keep a secret."

"I wouldn't go so far as to say that." I felt something warm and sticky. Glancing down at my hands, I could see the blood seep between my fingers. "Maybe you'd better not talk," I said.

"Maybe I had better talk," he replied. "In case I'm dying."

"You're not going to die," I assured him. "Neither side knows quite what to do with you yet."

"You might have a point," he said, coughing up a wad of blood. "But there's always purgatory."

"Go ahead and talk then," I said. "If you feel the need to."

He put his hand to his throat. His eyes looked a little distant. "I love her, you know. Rowena, that is." He coughed, spitting out another wad of blood. "I don't love much in this world, but I love her. That much I'm sure of."

"You went after Jimmy tonight," I pointed out.

"Who?" His eyes began to drift. He was losing consciousness.

"Jimmy. You went after him tonight when you didn't have to. And the other night when he ran away, you came after him then too. You must feel something for him."

He tried to shake his head, but my hands wouldn't let him.

201

"For Rowena's sake, not mine," he answered, closing his eyes. "And for her sake I'll try to raise him as my own."

"He is your own," I said before I could stop myself.

His eyes opened. "Who told you that?" he asked.

"Rowena told me yesterday. But it's supposed to be our secret."

I had to struggle to keep him still. "Why in the hell didn't she tell me?" he said.

"You'll have to take that up with her, but right now you need to rest. So relax," I said, seeing the headlights from Rupert's patrol car. "Help is on its way."

"Garth . . ." he said moments later after we loaded him into the backseat. "Is it really true that I'm Jimmy's father?"

"Yes, David, it's really true," said Rowena who had slipped into the car without his seeing her. She held his head in her lap.

"I'll be damned," he said with a smile just before he lost consciousness.

I closed the door on Rowena and him. "Ready," I said to Rupert.

"I'll get back as soon as I can," he replied.

I put my hand on his arm and said, "You'll play hell too. I can find my way home from here."

He left with his siren on and his lights flashing. We both knew that I wasn't going home.

20

Someone had blown the metal door off of Jimmy Parker's storeroom and taken nearly all of Jimmy's artifacts, leaving only a few arrowheads behind. The sharp smell of explosives still hung in the air, along with a blue haze that drifted spectrelike across the room, out the doorway, and into little Jimmy's bedroom. From there it slid slowly down the stairs and outside. Free at last! I thought to myself. All the ghosts imprisoned in that room were finally free at last.

I walked home to pick up my new flashlight and to tell Ruth where I was going. Then I backed Jessie out of the garage and left for the Barrens.

Tom Two-Feathers' Chevy pickup and Jimmy Parker's El Camino were parked next to the cabin where I'd spent the night with little Jimmy. I checked the engine just to make sure. It was still warm.

On my way to the cave, the wind pushed me along with a ferocity that made me stop, dig in my heels, and turn to confront it. Then I felt like a fool as it swept by me and continued on up the valley. I turned away from it once more and once more felt it hurrying me along. I hated to be hurried into anything almost as much as I hated anything that clung to me and wouldn't let go. That night, as it pushed me toward the mouth of the cave, I hated the wind as if it truly were a thing alive.

Once at the cave, I stopped long enough to catch my breath. Thinking back to the night that I stood there with a stick of dynamite in place, I wished that I had sealed the cave when I'd had the chance. It might not have changed anything. But at least I wouldn't have had to go back into it.

I went without a light for the first several yards because I already knew the way and I didn't want to attract anyone's attention. Gradually the wind began to die until finally I couldn't hear it anymore. But the silence that followed proved just as deafening as the wind.

When I could stand, I turned on the flashlight and followed it into the chamber where the cave divided into two separate branches. I'd been to the left and knew what lay there. Even if I'd known for certain that he'd taken Jimmy there, I wasn't sure if I could have made myself follow. The thought of traversing the pit again was more than I could bear. So with the hope that he'd taken Jimmy to the right, I went in that direction.

Like the left branch of the cave, the one on the right began to descend sharply once the two separated. Troll-like stalactites and stalagmites met in the middle of the cave, cutting off the flashlight's beam and narrowing the passage through which I walked. As I inched past the sharp-edged crystals that grew like double-rowed sharks' teeth along the sides of the cave, and then past the half dozen or so smaller tunnels that branched off from the main one, I found myself wishing that I'd brought along a ball of twine to unwind behind me.

Then I heard and smelled the river once again. Somewhere close at hand it flowed with a fury that seemed to match that of the wind outside. I pressed on, certain, and yet afraid, that this time I would find the

204

river—and that somewhere along its course I would encounter Jimmy Parker.

But I wasn't prepared for the river's full power and majesty, or for the spell that it cast over me once I reached its misty realm. As if it fed on tension and turbulence, sucking them from the air and spewing them out again upon the rocks and boulders in its path, the river cascaded between two steep, smooth banks that looked like walls of glass. I took a step toward it and felt my legs go limp, as fear rolled over me, like the gauzy fog along the river's edge. The river ran unbroken for as far as my mind could see. If I fell into it, I would never fall out.

I saw little Jimmy Parker long before he saw me. He was lying on a sheer quartz ledge and leaning precariously out over the river, trying to touch the water. I didn't dare call out to him for fear that I might startle him and make him lose his grip. Neither did I dare move too quickly toward him or I might fall into the river myself. Wet from the mist and the spray, the river's glassy banks were every bit as slippery as they looked.

I went a few feet, then saw Jimmy reach even lower, lose his balance point, and begin to slide slowly into the river. Unable to stop his slide, I could only scramble to where he was and grab one of his feet before he was sucked into the river.

Dropping my flashlight, I reached under me with my right hand, took the knife from my belt, and jabbed in hard into the bank. I expected its sharp slender point to break from the blow. Instead, it dug into the quartz bank like a diamond bit and held fast. Either the bank was not quartz, or whoever had made the knife had somehow tempered it to incredible hardness.

I held fast to Jimmy, the knife held fast to the bank, and gradually, what seemed like an inch at a time, I dragged both of us well up onto the glassy bank. Then I wrapped my legs around Jimmy to hold him and to

205

keep him away from the river, while I sheathed my knife and picked up the flashlight again.

"Okay, Jimmy," I said, rising and steadying myself, "Here we go." I swung him onto my shoulders. "Hold on tight."

He didn't have to be told twice. He held on so tightly I could hardly breathe as we started back along the bank in the direction I'd come. I made doubly sure of my footing before each step. This was unlike the day when I carried him out of the Barrens over the ice. Here we didn't have the luxury of falling then getting up again. One slip and we'd be into the river for all time.

"Don't look down," I said to Jimmy when he began to squirm. "And hold still. We'll be out of here in a minute."

But he wasn't looking down. He'd looked back over his shoulder instead. What he must have sensed rather than seen was the presence of someone following us.

I had two handicaps: Jimmy and the cavernous maze that lay ahead. While I had to find our way by flashlight, our pursuer already knew the route as well as a groundhog knew his own burrow. Alternately panting and wheezing, as if frustrated by the forces colliding with him, he closed to within a few yards of us and stayed there.

We entered a chamber where I had time only to drop Jimmy from my shoulders and unsheath my knife before I turned to shine my light in the face of our pursuer. He ducked from the light and covered his eyes until he could see again. Then, with his left hand held out in front of him and his right holding his own quartz knife, Jimmy Parker started toward us.

"Jimmy!" I shouted, hoping he'd stop.

But he kept advancing, while I backed away, dragging little Jimmy with me.

"Daddy, don't hurt us," little Jimmy pleaded. "Please don't hurt us!"

206

I'd backed to the wall of the cave and had nowhere else to go. "Get out of the way, Jimmy," I said, trying to set him aside.

"No," he said, grabbing ahold of my right leg and holding on. "I won't let you hurt my daddy."

"He's not your daddy," I said, unable to shake loose of him. "He's changed into someone else."

"He is my daddy," Jimmy insisted, clutching me ever tighter. "And you're not going to hurt him."

The next sequence of events happened so fast that days later I was still trying to understand it. Hearing a deep growl, I swung my flashlight in the direction of it and saw the stranger emerge from the left wing of the cave and come over our way.

Dumb with terror, little Jimmy dug his fingers into my leg and held on. I could only keep my light trained on the stranger in the hope that something would break. Finally, when the stranger had closed the distance between us to a few feet, something did break—the man who had once been Jimmy Parker.

He took a wild swipe at the stranger with his knife, then bolted for the left wing of the cave and disappeared. Instantly, with a grace that belied his great bulk, the stranger turned and followed Jimmy. I pried little Jimmy from my leg and carried him to the opening that led to the outside, then got down on my hands and knees and gave him the wildest horse ride of his life.

My legs were raw from my ankles to my knees by the time I heard the wind. It poured into the mouth of the cave and brought with it the sweet smell of spring. As soon as I could get my legs to work again, I lifted Jimmy onto my shoulders and started down the hill toward Jessie. Part way there I met Clarkie coming up the hill toward us.

"Hold it right there!" he shouted, shining a flashlight in my eyes.

"For God's sake, Clarkie," I shouted back. "It's Garth."

"What's that on your shoulders?" he asked as we approached.

"One very tired and scared boy. Will you take him home to his mother for me?"

"No!" Jimmy said. "I want to stay with you."

"You can't, Jimmy," I said, unlocking his arms from around my throat, but unable to break the grip of his legs. "Clarkie," I said, exasperated. "Do you think you could give me a hand here?"

Jimmy had made up his mind that he wasn't going to let go of me, and he fought Clarkie and me every step of the way. With a struggle, we finally managed to get Jimmy detached from me and attached to Clarkie, but Jimmy, continuing to fight, fell backward and hung there with his feet hooked under Clarkie's arms.

"Start walking," I said to Clarkie.

"I can't. He'll fall."

"Probably no more than once. He's a fast learner."

"Take him to the car at least," Clarkie begged. "Then we'll lock him in the backseat."

"We'll just have to do this all over again," I said. "And I'm not in the mood."

Reluctantly, Clarkie started down the hill. Jimmy still hung precariously by his feet, as his head bobbed along just a few inches above the ground.

"Clarkie!" I yelled after him.

He turned back hopefully.

"How's David Roberts doing?" I asked.

"I don't know," he answered. "They'd just taken him into surgery when I left."

"How did you know where to find me?"

He waited patiently for Jimmy to quiet down. "What was that, Garth?"

"How did you know I'd be here?" I repeated.

"Ruth put out the word." Clarkie started down the

208

hill. Jimmy apparently got his second wind and began to yell all the louder. I could hear him all the way to the car.

At the mouth of the cave I stopped a moment to rest. Though the wind didn't seem to blow as furiously as before, it had a bite to it that I hadn't felt earlier that night. It was likely turning to the north. If it kept on course, we'd probably have snow showers by morning.

A few feet into the cave I heard the sounds of someone on the inside headed out. Backing away has never been one of my favorite things to do, but those few feet that I had to back out of the cave, on shins already raw, seemed endless. When I finally did reach the outside where I could stand up again, I withdrew my knife and held it at the ready.

"Damn!" I heard the stranger say from inside the cave. I smiled with relief and put my knife away. Emerging from the cave into the moonlight, he took my hand, and I pulled him to his feet.

"You okay?" I asked.

"I'm sore as hell," he answered, rubbing his shins. "But I'm okay."

"What about Jimmy Parker?" I asked.

He shook his head. "He never made it past the pit."

"You're sure?"

"I'm sure."

He sat down in the mouth of the cave where he could better rub his shins. I sat down in a crevice facing him where I would be out of the wind. Together we watched the quarter moon, which had tipped over and rode face down across the sky.

"Rain's coming," he said.

"It looks like it." A tipped moon was supposed to mean rain. We sat a while longer. Then I said, "Want to tell me about it?"

"Tell you what?"

"Who you are, what you're doing in Oakalla."

209

He turned his gaze toward me. He had the deepest, blackest eyes I'd ever seen. But with his guard down I could at last see the warmth in them, and the compassion. "What does it matter who I am or what I'm doing here," he said. "Or whether I'm here on a mission, like you seem to want to believe, or an old man passing through town who fell right into the middle of something and decided to ride it out. What really matters is that a boy lost his father tonight, and maybe his future as well."

"And found one," I said, feeling the irony.

"How so?"

I told him.

"Well, then let's hope that David Roberts makes it."

"Yeah, let's hope so."

He scanned the sky, perhaps looking for the Seven Sisters, and Star Who Walks At Night. "What do you really think happened to Jimmy Parker in that cave?" he asked.

"To make him go mad?"

"Or whatever it was that happened to him. What did he see to make him go crazy? Was it the shape of his own fears, or something within the cave itself?

I studied him a moment. He seemed to have his own thoughts on the subject that he wasn't sharing with me.

"I'm afraid that's something we'll never know."

He continued to watch the sky, seeming to find pleasure in reading it, as I found pleasure in reading faces and clouds. Then he rose and dusted himself off. "There is another possible explanation. That Jimmy Parker didn't go crazy at all. That what set him off wasn't an imaginary fear, or whatever spirit might live in that cave, but his own greed for what he hoped to find there, and the very real fear of losing his son to someone else."

"So which one is it?" I asked.

210

He shrugged as if to say that it wasn't important and started down the hill.

"Aren't you going back inside the cave?" I asked.

"For what?"

"To look for the rest of Matatomah's treasure."

Avoiding me, he said, "No. I have what I came for."

"Jimmy's artifacts, you mean."

He took offense. "They don't belong to Jimmy Parker any more than the bones of your ancestors do."

I stretched out my legs, felt the wind at my back. "They don't belong to you either," I pointed out.

"I know. And I don't plan to keep them."

"What do you plan to do with them?"

"I haven't decided yet. But there is one thing you might consider," he said. "Jimmy Parker was in the construction business, with access to explosives and detonators. So he could have blown that door to his room as easily as I. All I would have had to do then was to follow him out here and do some shuffling once he went into the cave."

"Is that the way it happened?"

He wouldn't commit himself. "That's the way it could have happened."

We walked down into the valley where Jessie was parked beside his pickup. I noticed that once there he was in no hurry to leave. I thought I knew why.

"You plan to seal the cave, don't you?" I asked. "As soon as I'm gone from here."

"Yes," he answered. "I plan to seal the cave."

"You've seen what's there," I said. "Do you think you have the right to deny it not only to the people of our time but to all the generations to come? For that matter, do you think anyone has that right?"

He rummaged through his camper, searching for what he'd need to blow the cave. "It's because I've seen what's there," he said, "that I'm sealing it. Think about it, Ryland." He stopped rummaging long enough to

211

survey the valley. "Right about here is where the amusement park will go. Over there's a good place for the motels and condominiums, or whatever else they decide to build. With, of course, a layer of asphalt and concrete covering everything. Then the guided tours will start at the mouth of the cave and end at the pit, which will have a rail around it and a little metal sign pointing out the fact that a man once fell to his death there. As for the rest of the cave, I don't know, since I haven't seen it. But I do know one thing, Ryland. If you think your water's bad now, wait until you have a million people a year using it for their sewer."

"It doesn't have to be that way," I argued.

"No," he said, his eyes black and hard. "But it usually is."

He continued to search through the back of his camper. I'd have given a lot to see what all was inside there. "That's not it," I said at last. "Those aren't your reasons for blowing the cave. They would be mine, but they aren't yours."

He stopped rummaging in the camper and stepped out into the moonlight. "What are my reasons then?"

"There's only one reason that I can think of," I said. "I saw it in your eyes there in the Corner Bar and Grill after you came back from the Barrens. It gave you new life and purpose and made you feel young again. You found something wonderful there. That's why you were gone for three days. You waited here for Jimmy Parker to leave, which he did Wednesday night, so that you could explore the cave in his absence. Then when you found whatever it was you found, you came back to Oakalla to see what might happen next. Perhaps you wanted a chance at Jimmy's artifacts, or perhaps you were just curious to see how it all turned out. It doesn't matter whether you went to Jimmy's house to take his artifacts, or you just happened to be in the neighborhood. When you saw Jimmy take little Jimmy tonight

212

and bring him back here, you had a choice. You could either take the artifacts and leave or try to save little Jimmy. You chose to save little Jimmy."

He laughed at me. "Ryland, you tell a good story."

"Then you didn't find something wonderful in that cave?"

His eyes shone with delight. He couldn't hide what he'd seen. "Say that I did find something wonderful. Say that I found relics unlike any I've ever seen before, or will see again. Whose worth is not something you can measure in time or money, but in the things themselves, the beauty of their design and the genius of the hands who made them." For a moment, he was somewhere back in the cave again, and several moments passed in which he didn't even know that I was there. "If I did make such a find, wouldn't I be honor bound to preserve it, Ryland? Wouldn't you? Don't you think that out of all the bounty of this earth . . . Don't you think that some things are sacred and should remain untouched? That they don't belong to you or me or my people or your people or the ages past or the ages to come? They belong to their creator. And should be preserved out of respect for him."

We stood a handshake apart. I had asked all the questions I had wanted to ask. He had told me all that he was going to. Then I reached into my sheath and tried to hand him the knife. "Here," I said. "You've earned it."

But he wouldn't take it. "So have you," he replied. "Many times over."

"All the more reason to give it to you then," I said, laying it in his palm.

His thick fingers slowly embraced it. "Then give me the sheath as well," he said.

"It didn't come with the knife. It's mine, left over from my childhood. It has no value except to me."

He looked through me to something beyond. "All

the more reason for me to have it. To remember you by."

I took the sheath off my belt and handed it to him. "You won't throw it back into the cave, or give it away to someone else?" I said, wanting his promise. "The knife, I mean."

"Only to my son at my death." His eyes turned away from me. "Or to yours, if you choose."

"I have no son to give it to," I said.

"You will someday," he assured me.

"Then have your son pass it on to mine on his twenty-first birthday."

He took my hand in his, as his huge fingers swallowed mine. "Done," he said.

I opened Jessie's door and was about to get inside when I had a sudden thought. "You're not in it for the money either, are you?" I said.

He smiled at me for the first time. "No, I'm not in it for the money."

Satisfied, I drove away.

21

Rupert, leading little Jimmy by the hand, got off the hospital elevator just as I was about to get on. I couldn't read Rupert's face because it was perpetually solemn, but his eyes seemed to be smiling. "How's David," I asked.

"He'll live" was his answer. "Now we're on our way to get a pop. Would you like one?"

"If you don't have a beer handy."

"I don't."

"Then I'd like a Dr Pepper."

Rupert made a face. "That stuff will rot your insides."

"I know. That's why I like it."

We found the pop machine, got a Pepsi for Rupert and Jimmy and a Dr Pepper for me, and sat down with our drinks. I could tell by the look on Jimmy's face that while things were better than a few hours before, all was still not quite right with him.

"Where's my daddy?" Jimmy asked. "He should be here too."

Rupert and I exchanged glances. He wanted to know too where Jimmy Parker was. "Your daddy fell into the river," I said.

215

He pondered a moment, then asked, "Is he coming back?"

I shook my head. "No."

"Is he dead?" he asked.

"Yes, Jimmy, he's dead," I answered.

"Is he in heaven?"

I looked to Rupert for help but didn't see any forthcoming. "I don't know, Jimmy. That's not up to me."

Out of questions for the moment, he went back to drinking his Pepsi.

"I suppose now's not the time for an explanation," Rupert said.

"No," I agreed. "It isn't."

A week into April we had our first thunderstorm of the year. It lit up the sky for over an hour, shook the house and rattled the windows, and washed the last black piles of snow down the drain. Ruth and I sat at the breakfast table the morning after the storm with cups of coffee in our hands, the Sunday paper spread out between us, and the remains of breakfast drying on our plates. For the first time in a month the coffee tasted good enough for a second and third cup, and for the first time in a month, Oakalla's water had been given the green light by the State Board of Health.

Leaning back in my chair, I watched a couple of robins gorging themselves on earthworms and nightcrawlers. For them life had become fat after the storm, the crawlers and worms easy pickings. But after the March that they'd put in, they deserved some easy pickings. For that matter, we all did.

I sorted through the paper, found a section that I hadn't read, then noticed Ruth giving me the evil eye. "I suppose this is the very section you wanted," I said.

"It is," she answered. "But that's beside the point."

I searched my memory for anything that I might

216

have done to offend her recently, but came up empty. "I give up," I said. "What have I done now?"

"You've gone a week without asking me about Thorton's personal papers."

I scanned the editorial section of the paper to see if anybody had anything new to say. "I figured those letters were your business," I said. "Seeing how they were all addressed to you."

"They are my business," she replied, trying to stare me down. "That's why I wonder why you haven't said anything. Since you usually make my business your business at every opportunity."

"Meaning?" I asked, already knowing what she meant.

"Meaning you've probably already read them."

I held up both hands and said, "I swear I haven't. But even if I had, I gave you first dibs at them if I remember right."

"I know that," she snapped, snatching the entertainment section out from in front of me. "I just didn't know how personal they'd be. I mean after fifty years you'd think he would have run out of ways to say how much he loved me."

"Some people never run out of ways."

"Do you really think he did?"

I watched two robins wrestle with the same worm. Even with the yard full of worms, each wanted what the other had. "Did what?" I asked.

"Love me for all that time?"

"I think he thought he did. It amounts to the same thing."

She sighed and leaned back in her chair. She had a faraway look in her eyes. "I never knew," she said.

"Would it have mattered if you did?"

"I don't know. Maybe after Karl died."

"Are you sure? You had your chance, remember? You sent him packing before he ever got to first base."

"I might not have if I'd read those letters of his ahead of time."

I smiled at her. "Want to bet?"

She came back to life. "No." She began to read the entertainment section. "I don't want to bet."

Rupert knocked on the front door. I left Ruth sitting at the table and went to answer it. "I can't stay," he said, stepping just inside the door. "I promised Elvira I'd take her and the rest of the family to church this morning."

"How's the rest of your family getting along?" I asked.

He reached into his pocket for his tobacco pouch, then thought better of it. "Not bad, under the circumstances. David's on the mend, and Rowena took down the For Sale sign in her yard until she and David figure out what they want to do with their lives." He frowned. "I hope it's soon. It seems that's all David has done for most of his life—try to figure out what to do with it."

"Maybe now that David's married he will."

"Maybe," he said, adjusting the brim of his hat before he put it back on. "But I'm not holding my breath."

"Don't leave without this," I said, picking up a small greasy leather suitcase from beside the door and handing it to him. It was the same suitcase that Edgar and I had taken from the trunk of Stub's old Buick Roadmaster. "It's all there, except for the price of a new camera lens and the two hundred dollars I gave Edgar Shoemaker for services rendered."

He whistled. "Edgar's rates must have gone up."

"Well, there were two different jobs involved, one a door and the other the trunk of a car."

"I think I'd rather not hear about it." Then he shook the suitcase a couple times. "How much do you figure is in here?"

"Enough to clean up Stub's mess."

218

"What about leftovers, if there are any?"

I followed him outside to his patrol car. "I'll leave that up to you."

He put the suitcase in the trunk and got into the patrol car. "Clarkie and I made a trip out to that cave the day before yesterday," he said. "Or where Clarkie thought it was. But somebody had sealed it up tighter than a drum. We couldn't find either entrance." He glanced up at me. "You wouldn't happen to know anything about that, would you?"

"No," I answered.

"That's what I figured," he said. He gazed at the street, still wet from the overnight rain. "You know, we haven't done a thing to clean up that mess over in the Barrens. Somehow the water cleared up on its own."

"Given the opportunity, sometimes it does," I answered.

"I thought maybe you knew something I didn't."

"Not in this case."

Continuing to stare at the street, he watched a couple of sparrows taking a bath in a mud puddle. "What was the cave like, Garth? I'd really like to know."

"Have you ever been to Carlsbad Caverns?" I asked.

"Once. Years ago."

"Something like that," I said. "Only better."

"Was there really a river down there?"

"Yes."

"What else?"

I started to tell him, then stopped. What I'd seen and felt down there was too close to me to share, even with him. "You'd have to see it for yourself."

He started the car. "There's not much chance of that, is there?" As the car crept forward, he said, "I see you lost your knife."

I touched my belt where I had carried it. For a panic-stricken moment I thought I had lost it until I

219

remembered what I'd done with it. "I didn't lose it," I answered. "I gave it away."

He stopped the car. "The stranger?" he asked.

I nodded.

"Figures." He drove on.

I watched him go, then put my hand on my belt where the knife had hung. With it in my possession, I had felt invincible, the true son of Matatomah and the ancients who once roamed Oakalla. Without it, I was merely Garth Ryland, owner and editor of the *Oakalla Reporter*, and not even a native son of Wisconsin. I felt the loss in spirit and stature. But not so keenly, since the stranger had promised me my own son one day.